SOUTHERN PLANTATION

STORIES AND SKETCHES

"Uncle Alex and Aunt Rachel."

SOUTHERN PLANTATION
STORIES AND SKETCHES

By
GEORGE E. WILEY

The Black Heritage Library Collection

 BOOKS FOR LIBRARIES PRESS
FREEPORT, NEW YORK
1971

First Published 1905
Reprinted 1971

INTERNATIONAL STANDARD BOOK NUMBER:
0-8369-8836-1

LIBRARY OF CONGRESS CATALOG CARD NUMBER:
78-161277

PRINTED IN THE UNITED STATES OF AMERICA

SOUTHERN

PLANTATION STORIES
AND SKETCHES

BY

GEORGE E. WILEY, M.D.

BRISTOL, VA.

Member of The American Medical Association and
Medical Society of Virginia.

ILLUSTRATIONS BY

FRANK S. DIXON

NEW YORK

NEW YORK
1905

Press of J. J. Little & Co.
Astor Place, New York

THESE STORIES ARE DEDICATED

TO THE

OLD EMORY AND HENRY COLLEGE BOYS

WITH

AFFECTIONATE REMEMBRANCE

OF THE HAPPY DAYS WE SPENT THERE TOGETHER

AND THE TALES WE HAVE HEARD

FROM OLD UNCLE HARVY KING

AND WESLEY WOODSON

CONTENTS

		PAGE
	PUBLISHERS' NOTE	5
	PREFACE	11
I	UNCLE ALEX AND THE MULE . . .	13
II	UNCLE PHIL'S VISIT TO HEAVEN . . .	29
III	UNCLE FRED AND THE YELLOW JACKETS .	35
IV	THE CORN SHUCKING	41
V	THE SNAKE CHARMER	53
VI	HOW THE LITTLE BOY GOT FRIGHTENED AT THE CANDLE MOULDS	61
VII	HOW THE LITTLE BOYS BROKE UP A REVIVAL	65
VIII	THE CABIN IN THE WOODS	73
IX	THE BLIND FIDDLER	83
X	AN ADVENTURE	93
XI	WHIPPED INTO MANHOOD	103
XII	THE MEANEST MAN IN THE WORLD . .	121

PUBLISHERS' NOTE

THE Publishers of this volume of negro dialect stories and sketches wish to say that it is unique in that the author is the first person since the war between the North and South that has undertaken the great and humane task of providing local homes for the old, worn out ex-slaves in the Southern States.

He has started a movement by which he hopes to secure such a home in Southwest Virginia. The plan is to purchase a few hundred acres of land suitable for agricultural purposes, truck gardening, poultry raising, etc.

Employment thus giving to those able to work which will pay their way all or in part, and at the same time teach the children that are old enough how to farm, garden, cook, and such other practical information as may be valuable to them and others in afterlife, while they get the rudiments of an education.

This plan has met with the endorsement of many of the leading men of Virginia as the following letters will attest.

Gov. A. J. Montague writes in part:

" I am interested in your project and trust you may have such co-operation in establishing the home for old, worn out ex-slaves and orphan negro children in Southwest Virginia as your meritorious enterprise deserves."

Ex-Governor J. Hague Tyler says in part:

" I must say I approve most heartily of your plan to establish some kind of a home for the worn out ex-slaves and orphan negro children of that race in Southwest Virginia. Nothing more appropriate could be conceived of than to build a home for the aged and for the orphaned and helpless children that are found among them in such large numbers. I pray that God may speed your good work."

Judge Jno. A. Buchanan of the Supreme Court of Appeals says:

" I heartily approve of your scheme to build a home for old, worn out ex-slaves and orphan negro children in Southwest Virginia. The people, both North and South, who feel an interest in the welfare of their country, fear the dangers which threaten it from ignorance and vice, and desire to see the orphans of an unfortunate race cared for and reared so as to fit them for the duties of life, and cannot but approve the noble and humane object proposed."

Charles E. Vawter, President of the Miller Manual Labor School of Virginia, writes in part:

6

" I am president of the Virginia Society of Chari-
ties and Corrections, and I feel so deeply interested
in what you propose to do that I hope to enlist (as
I know I can) the Society in this great work. You
speak the keynote when you say, help them to help
themselves. This tells it all. You will add to their
happiness, their hope, their heaven, by so doing."

Hon. Daniel Trigg writes in part:

" I can conceive of no more exalted and worthy
charity. It is deserving because the people whom
you would help are comparatively helpless. It is the
cause of humanity. God grant that you may succeed
in this undertaking."

Judge F. B. Hutton, of the Twenty-third Judicial
Circuit, writes:

" I most sincerely and earnestly endorse any
scheme that will make the old ex-slaves' declining
years more comfortable. The people of the United
States who feel an interest in the welfare of their
country must feel an increasing anxiety over the
dangers that threaten it arising from ignorance and
vice, and the training of the orphan negroes on the
lines you propose would meet the approval of all
classes of our citizens."

Dr. Robert J. Preston, Superintendent of the
Southwestern State Hospital, writes in part:

" I approve most cordially this movement. When
I remember the faithfulness of the negroes during the

7

Civil War, I feel that a monument should be erected to their memory. Nothing could be more appropriate than the plan you propose, and by taking the orphans of such ex-slaves and training them, thus the present evil tendencies might be counteracted and their former love and friendship for the whites fostered and cultivated."

Congressman W. P. Brownlow writes in part:

"I am glad to know you are interested in building a home for ex-slaves in Southwest Virginia. Your cause is certainly a very commendable one and I hope for your success."

T. W. Jordan, Dean and Professor of Latin in the University of Tennessee, writes in part:

"Your effort to provide a refuge for ex-slaves no longer able to take care of themselves, meets my hearty approval. In it you have the sympathy of all who lived among them. Any help given them, especially means by which they can partially help themselves, is a most commendable charity and I earnestly wish you success."

Joseph D. Jarman, President of the State Female Normal School of Virginia, writes in part:

"I cheerfully endorse the idea of building a home for old, worn out ex-slaves and orphan negro children in Southwest Virginia. With reference to orphan negro children, I will add that both from a standpoint of humanity as well as from a consideration of the best interest of the State, they should be cared for and trained along industrial lines, which would tend to make them law-abiding citizens rather than vagrants. You certainly deserve to succeed in such a work of charity as well as constructive philanthropy."

R. G. Waterhouse, President of Emory and Henry College, writes in part:

" I believe an institution, such as you contemplate and intend to serve first of all the needy ex-slaves and their needy orphan descendants in East Tennessee and Southwest Virginia, would prove a great blessing to the negro, and be such an expression of humane interest in his welfare as his past history merits, and as the best people of this section undoubtedly feel."

United States Senator John W. Daniel writes in part:

" I would like to see you succeed in the home for worn out ex-slaves and orphan colored children. An institution of this sort, well managed and cared for, would do much good."

The proceeds from the sale of this book, above cost of publication, will be devoted to the purpose of assisting in carrying out this humane enterprise which seems to us eminently appropriate.

We bespeak for the volume a large sale.

PREFACE

IN presenting to the public this little book of Short Stories I have had two ends in view: First, to entertain the children. Second, to record some of the old ante-bellum negroes' dialect, phrases, idioms, and shrewd imagery, which, in ten years hence, will have passed with him.

"Like his master, the ex-slave has grown hoary in the struggle to meet new conditions, but unlike his master he has not been able to conquer. Worn with the struggle he drops out of life, with no successor in his race, no bequeathment of himself to history except through the dialect story of the South.

"With him passes also that unique relation between master and slave which preserved the old wine of bondage in the new bottles of the nineteenth century and left a peculiar cordiality between the two after emancipation."

The dialect stories in this book are all true, and recorded, as I remember them, from the lips of the old colored friends of the days of my youth, many of whom have passed away. In memory I can see their shadowy forms, and hear their tuneful voices.

The other stories are all based on facts, being therefore more truth than fiction.

11

Many of the faces in the book are genuine pictures taken from photographs furnished the artist who made the illustrations. I have no apology to offer for the imperfections it contains; indeed, its very imperfections is a kind of recommendation, for it has been written more to entertain children than " grown up people," and naturalness has been aimed at rather than rhetoric, and if I succeed in entertaining for an hour the boys and girls on rainy days and long winter evenings, and make the hours shorter to the sick ones while mother reads these stories aloud, my aim has been accomplished.

These stories will be especially interesting to city children inasmuch as they portray a phase of country life which they have not seen, and never will see, because the old-time negro will have become a matter of legendary history before they become men and women.

In the story of " Whipped Into Manhood," the part in regard to the bear hunt has been partially told by my old friend, Chas. B. Cole, in his book of the life of Wilburn Walters, an Indian hermit, hunter and trapper; but in this book it is as I have heard him relate it when a boy sitting on his knee. The characters in this story are all genuine and still living, except the old Indian, who has long since joined his fathers on the Happy Hunting grounds.

THE AUTHOR.

UNCLE ALEX AND THE MULE

DURING the war the Yankees came along and took away every one of our horses, and left an old army mule with U. S. branded on his shoulder. This old mule was the only thing we had, in the way of horse power, to work in the corn field or elsewhere. This sole dependence seemed very slim, for he was so poor that he could hardly walk and was besides lame in his left hind foot. Some said he had the " foot evil." However that may have been, one thing was certain, he had an evil foot; for he could do more with his hind feet than any living creature I ever saw.

Although this mule was in such a forlorn condition when left at our house, it was not very long before he began to pick up a little, and, when he heard anyone coming, he would lift up his ears, but they would not stay up, they would flop down again. This up-and-down movement of his ears was the first sign he showed of feeling any better. A curious fact about him was, that his eyes did not share in his abject appearance, but always looked very bright, even from the first.

The little boy said one day that he was going to take the U. S. off his shoulder; for the neighbors said that if the Federals came along and saw that they would take him away from us, and that, too, when it would be corn planting time. Aunt Rachel said, " Honey, how is yo' gwine ter git it off?" The little boy said, " Why, Aunt Rachel, don't you know how to do that?" She said, " No, honey, I don't know how yo' is gwine ter git dem scars off dat mule's shoulder; dey is done been burnt in dar." The little boy said, " Well, Aunt Rachel, I am going to burn them out. I am going to rub it with turpentine and set it on fire." She said, " Honey, what yo' think dat mule is er gwine ter do while yo' is settin' him on fire?" He replied, " Why, mammy, he can't hold his ears up; how can he hurt me?" " All right, honey; don't rub too much on fust. Rub it on whar de letters is, fur I knows we is boun' to git dem letters off dar some way." So the little boy rubbed turpentine on the letters, and the mule stood quietly as if he was asleep—he liked to be rubbed. After he got the turpentine on, he lighted a piece of paper and started out in the yard. When he got to the door with the burning paper, the mule lifted his ears; but about that time the paper went out, and just as soon as the fire disappeard, his ears flopped down again. He had evidently formed a dislike to fire, when they put that U. S. brand on his shoulder. Aunt Rachel

14

said, " I spec' yo' had better wait 'till Uncle Alex
comes in fo' yo' tries ter set dat mule on fire, kaze I
don't lek de way he lif' his ears up and switch his
tail, when yo' started out wid dat fire. " O, he won't
do anything, Aunt Rachel, he won't know it 'till I
light it, then I will run in the house." She said,
" All right, honey." The little boy got a pine stick
this time, lighted it, and when he got to the door, the
mule lifted up his ears again and began to switch his
tail. When the little boy got out on the ground, the
mule gave one look at the fire, walked up to the picket
fence, drew that sore foot up, and hopped over the
fence on three legs into the garden, just as easy as a
cat could jump a broom stick, and never touched the
fence with his sore foot. Aunt Rachel said, " Now,
don't dat beat de Dutch. Dat mule knows fire wen
he sees it, an' he standin' roun' yere lek he wuz
mighten nigh dead, and jump dat picket fence jis'
as easy as I can go through de gate. Yo' let dat
mule 'lone, honey, till Alex comes, kaze he aint er
gwine ter let yo' tech him wid fire, if he kin help it.
Dat mule has done showed his disprobation fur fire,
an' is dun showed he aint as nigh dead as he lets on;
and 'sides dat, he will tramp de garden all to pieces.
Come in de house, honey; de mule is dun showed he
aint er gwine to have his U. S. took off wid fire. Yo'
have to take it off some yuther way. Come on in,
honey, kaze if yo' don't, I is er gwine ter tell ole

15

Mistes. Dat mule is sholy not er gwine to 'ject his self ter fire."

About this time Uncle Alex came in from the field and said, " Look yere, Rachel, wat's dat mule doin' in de garden ? " Rachel told Uncle Alex what had happened. Uncle Alex said, " Well, I declar to gracious, I never thought dat mule could jump dat garden fence."

He went in and took him by the foretop and led him out at the gate, and the mule hopped along on three feet, and stumbled over a stick of wood, and came near falling down. Aunt Rachel said, " I declar to goodnes, dat mule lettin' on lek he can't scacly walk, an' he dun jumped dat picket fence des' de same as any deer. Well, honey dat beats my time." Uncle Alex led the mule up to the stable lot that had a high rail fence around it, and turned him in. The mule stood in the corner of the fence with his ears dropped down, holding up his sore foot like it was giving him great pain.

The little boy watched the mule a long time, and at last, he went to the house and said, " Mammy, give me one of those sulphur matches you have been saving so long." She said, " No sir-ree, yo' pintedly is not gwine ter git nary one of dem matches, kaze when dem matches is gone, we is got to keep a fire burnin' all de time, fur if de matches is all gone and de fire all goes out, how in de name of de Laud er we

gwine ter git any mo' fire started? No sir, I can't
give yo' nary one of dem matches, ef de Yankees do
come an' git dat ole mule. He ain't no 'count no
how, an' I ain't had no peace er min' since dat ole
mule come on dis place; an' 'sides dat, even if he
wuz, yo' knows well as I does, dat mule aint gwine
ter let yo' tech him wid no match. I is dun seed dat."
But all the time she was rummaging around in a box
to find the matches, for she knew and so did the little
boy, that she was going to give him the match. So
sure enough, the old woman got the match and said,
"Now dars dat match, an' mek de mos' uv it, fur I
is not er gwine ter give yo' no mo' matches fur
nothin'."

The little boy took the match, and slipping up to
the fence right quietly, lit it, and stuck his hand
through the crack in the fence, and touched it to the
turpentine spot on the mule's shoulder. It flashed
into a blaze at once, and the mule just went around
the lot once, then drew up his sore foot, and over the
rail fence he went, never touching it, and around the
field he galloped, the turpentine blazing, until at
last he lay down and wallowed, and thus put the fire
out. Uncle Alex and Aunt Rachel were standing in
the yard watching. At last Aunt Rachel said, "I
declar befo' de Laud, dat boy an' dat mule beats
anything I's eber seed befo' in my life. Ef anybody
had tole me dat boy could set dat mule on fire, an'

dat mule could jump dat stake an' rider fence wid three legs, an' den stinquish de fire on his own self, I would not er believed it, but I dun seed him do it wid my own eyes. Dat certainly is a 'markable mule."

Every day Uncle Alex would wash and grease the mule's burnt shoulder, and he would stand as still as a mouse, with his ears flopped down. After a while his burn got entirely well, the U. S. had disappeared from his shoulder, and he began to get some flesh on his bones. But there was one thing you could not do,—keep him in any lot or field he did not want to stay in. Uncle Alex said he could "stand and jump any fence he could put his nose over, and run and jump over the moon, if it had a fence around it."

One day Uncle Alex said he was going to plough corn with the mule; he was plenty able to work if he could jump the way he did. So he put a bridle on him, hitched him to the fence and went into the stable and got the harness. When the mule saw him coming with it, he lifted up his ears and began to switch his tail. When Uncle Alex got close to him, he began to jump and kick, and Uncle Alex could not get anywhere near him, but if he would lay the harness down on the ground he could go up to him. He would drop his ears and look like he was asleep. Uncle Alex said, " Ef dat aint de banginest mule

18

eber I seed in my life, my name aint Alex White.
What's I gwine ter do wid yo'? Yo' knows I's got
ter plough cone wid yo', or dar won't be no cone for
yo' ter eat, an' yo' can't pull no plough widout dem
gears on yo'. Now what yo' gwine ter do 'bout it?"
The little boy said: "Uncle Alex, you see what
he is going to do about it, but what are you going to
do about it?" Uncle Alex said, "Now look yere,
honey, what's yo' axin' me foolish questions fur?
Yo' knows Alex well 'nuf ter know what he's gwine
ter do. He is er gwine ter put dem gears on dat mule
an' plough dat cone wid him, ceptin' he die fo' I gits
de gears on him; dat's Alex, honey, an' yo' knows
hit."

About this time Aunt Rachel came up and said,
"I dunno 'bout dat Alex, I dunno 'bout dat. When
I seed yo' jes' now, dat mule wuz on de pint er kickin' yo' brains out, an' a mule what kin jump as high
as dat mule is not er gwine ter have no gears on dis
time ob day, now, yo' mark what Rachel dun tole
yo'." "Now look e yere, Rachel; yo' knows I don't
'low no wimmen come foolin' 'long wid my bizness;
sides dat, yo' is dun tuck sides wid dat mule, an' hit
don't s'prise me ter heah yo' talk dat way; but yo'
watch Alex, dats all I'se got ter say." He led the
mule up in a corner of the fence by the side of an old
apple tree, got a long pole and put up by the side of
him so that the mule could not get out, then he got

up on the fence and dropped the harness down on his back. Of all the kicking you ever saw done, that mule did it. He had the harness off on the ground in less time than it takes to tell it. Uncle Alex had to take the pole down and let the mule out, to get the harness.

The little boy said, " Uncle Alex, what are you going to do now ? " Uncle Alex said, " Now what's yo' keep on er axin' me dat fur ? It's ' Uncle Alex what's yo' gwine ter do now ? What's yo' gwine ter do now ? ' Yo' knows what I's er gwine ter do now, an' what I's er gwine ter do all de time. I's er gwine ter ride dat mule, jes' what I said I wuz gwine ter do all de time, honey. I's er gwine ter ride him; yo' heard me say so frum de fust startin' uv it. Dat mule is done bin yere fur two munts, an' aint dun narry lick uv wuck yit. He may rip, an' he may rare, and kick, but taint no use. I's er gwine ter ride him. He's jes bin standin' roun' yere, wid his ears flopped down, an' he lips hung down, lettin' on lek' he is sick, an' he aint bin sick narry minit; he aint, in my 'pinion, bin feelin' bad. He's not er gwine ter fool ole Alex no mo'.''

Uncle Alex went in the stable and brought out the old army saddle that the Yankees had left, when they took away the horses. He got the mule again and led him up to where the saddle lay on the ground. Everything went all right up to this point, except

20

the mule seemed to pay some attention to the saddle lying on the ground. But when Alex stooped down to pick up the saddle, by some twist of that lame hind foot, he managed to hit Alex on the seat of his pants, landing him about five feet away on the top of his head. When Alex picked himself up, the mule was standing quietly by the saddle just as if nothing had happened. Language seemed to have deserted Alex for the time being, at least he did not seem able to express himself, for he just stood looking at the mule. It seemed to the little boy that Uncle Alex grew larger than he was before the mule kicked him. It must have been true, for Aunt Rachel, when she got her breath from laughing, said, " Alex, what yo' standin' dar fur, swelled up lek a garden toad, an' lookin' at dat mule ? Is yo' dun loss yo' speech, or is dat mule dun tuck de breff outen yo' ? I 'clare to gracious dat mule handle dat lame hin' foot wid great 'gility."

By this time Alex's power of utterance had returned and he said, " Rachel, I thought yo' did hab sum sense, an' sum manners, an' heah yo' is talkin' to me 'bout bein' swelled up lek a garden toad an' er mirin' dat mule in de use uv he hin' foot, an' Alex mighten nigh killed. I 'clare to de Laud, I believe yo' an dat mule is in cahoot, kaze I aint neber seed nuthin' dun lek dat befo'." No, Alex, bress de Laud, yo' aint seed dat yit, kaze yo' aint got no eyes behin' yo', but I seed it, Alex, an' it suttenly is cu'ous how dat mule handle dat foot."

By this time the mule had walked off, and began cropping the grass. Uncle Alex got the saddle and laid it in the stable, pausing once or twice to look at the mule, as though trying to understand how he kicked him when he was not behind him.

On the following morning the little boy said, " Uncle Alex, I thought you were going to plough the old mule. Uncle Alex said, " Lawd, honey, I ain't studyin' 'bout no mule." " Well, Uncle Alex, aint you going to ride the mule? " Alex replied, " Aint I dun tole yo', I aint studyin' 'bout no mule." " Well, Uncle Alex, what are you studyin' about? " " I's studyin' 'bout dem Yankees what lef' dat mule here; what in de name of de Lawd dey think we gwine ter do wid him, an' what yo' dun tuck de U. S. off en him fur? Dat mule don't long here, an' de suner de Yankees comes an' gits him, de better hit will be fur dat mule, kase I's gwine ter kill him; yo' hear me don' yo? I's er gwine ter kill him sho'. " " Uncle Alex, don't kill him; I will tell you how to ride him." " How kin yo' ride him, honey? " " Why get on him without the saddle. He lets you rub him, and put the bridle on him, and he won't do anything if you get on his bare back." " Well, if he won't let de saddle ride, wat yo' think he gwine let Alex ride fur? No, no, honey, he done fool Alex

once, he not gwine ter fool Alex agin, not if Alex
knows hisself." "Well, Uncle Alex, I will get on
him." "All right, honey, yo' kin try hit ef yo' wants
to, but in 'cordance wid my 'pinion, yo' is in danger.
Yo' kin b'lieve me er not b'lieve des as yo' min' ter,
but dat ar long flop-yeared creetur, dat ar up en
down, an' sailin' roun', 'ceitful creetur, wat one minit
can't lif' his foot over er stick er wood, an' den lif'
'is whole body over dat ar stake, an' ride fence, an'
neber tech a har, is dangus to fool wid. Now yo' is
dun heerd all Alex got ter say. Let 'lone dat,
aint yo' dun seed him kick Alex, an' Alex not er
standin' hin' 'im? A mule what kin kick yo' an yo'
standin' in front uv 'im, dar aint no pendance to be
put in 'im, an' dis ol' nigger tell yo' right now, he
aint gwine ter have nothin' mo' ter to do wid 'im,
an' to tell yo' de Lawd's trufe, honey, yo' 'ud better
take my 'dvice an' stay clean 'way from dat mule."
"Well, Uncle Alex, I know he will let me rub him;
he don't mind my coming close to him. I don't think
he will do anything, if I haven't got the saddle."

"All right, honey, yo' kin try hit, but Alex aint
er gwine ter have nuthin' ter do wid it, an' ef my
eye aint 'ceive me, dat mule know yo' is talkin' 'bout
'im right dis minit."

"Well, I am going to try it anyhow, Uncle Alex."
"Tooby sho', honey, tooby sho', yo' kin try hit, but
I 'low yo' better be gittin' ready to say yo' pra'rs

23

fust, kaze dat mule aint gwine ter 'low yo' ter git on 'im; now yo' min' wat I's dun tol' yo'."

But the little boy went up to the old mule, rubbed his ears and his nose, and patted him on the side, and led him up to the fence; then he climbed up on the fence and got on his back right easy, and the old mule stood as still as a stone. Alex watched the proceedings with great interest, and when he saw that the mule was not going to cut any capers, he said, " Dis ole nigger's dun bin al' ober dis whole worl' and clear down to de fur een' er no whar, an' dun bin chase' by de patter rollers, but in all er my trabels, I aint seed nuthin' like dat mule. Git down ofen dar, honey, an' let Alex on dar, an' les' see wat he er gwine ter do, wen I gits on 'im, fur yo' dun heerd me say long er go, I wuz er gwine ter ride dat mule, cuttin' up er no cuttin' up. He kin rip en he kin rar, but I's er gwine ter ride 'im, an' I 'low dis is er mighty good time fer ter do it. Git down, honey, an' let Uncle Alex on dar, dat hoppity, skippity, up-en-down, en sailin' roun' aint er gwine ter do no good now; Alex is er gwine ter ride."

The little boy slid off the mule, and Alex approached him very cautiously, walking all around him and looking at his hind legs especially. Finally he went up in front of him, put out his hand and touched him on the nose, then jumped back, and said, " Wo dar, I tell yo', I don't want none yo' foolish-

"'Now I's er gwine ter put dat saddle on yer.'"

ness." The mule had never moved a muscle. He approached him again, put his hand on his foretop and said, " Wo, I tell yo'; yo' kin look befo' yo', an' yo' kin look behin' yo', an' yo' kin look all 'roun yo' ef yo' wants to, but Alex is right here, an' he's gwine ter ride yer."

He led the mule up to the fence just as the little boy had done, and with great caution settled himself on the mule's back. The mule stood perfectly still. The little boy handed him a switch, and he whipped the mule furiously until it moved off a few steps and began cropping the grass, just as it had done with the little boy. The old negro said, " Oh yes, haint I tol' yo', it wuz no use rarin', an' takin' on so, 'bout hit; haint I dun tol' yo' Alex gwine ter ride yo' 'fore he dun wid yo'; an' sides, I's er gwine ter show yo' how to cut up, an' kick, an' rar roun', an' jump fences, an' kick Unc. Alex wen he eye not on yer."

The old man got down and said, " Now I's er gwine ter put dat saddle on yer, an' take some co'n ter mill. I boun' I show yo' how to tote yo'self 'bout dis place." He went in the stable and came out with the saddle and approached the mule with very little caution, when almost as quick as a flash the mule whirled and kicked with both feet at the old negro, fortunately striking the saddle he had in front of him, but knocking him heels over head. It was some minutes before he was able to speak. Then he said, " Des like I dun tell yo', honey; dar aint no creetur wat kin stan' right flat footed an wuk he min' quick lek a mule. He dun 'lowed yo' ter ride 'im, an' he dun 'lowed me ter ride, des so he cud git ter kick me wen I cum wid de saddle, an' now he's dun busted dis saddle, till taint fitten to put on nuthin', an' how in de name ob de Lawd is I gwine ter ride on dat saddle now? Cum on way from dar, honey, an' let dat mule 'tent hisself wid bustin' de saddle."

About this time Rachel appeared in the kitchen door and said, " Alex, cum on yer to yo' dinner, yo' triflin' black nigger; yo' aint cut no stove wood to-day. Yo' is always er foolin' 'bout dat stable, 'stead cuttin' wood fur me ter cook wid. I 'clare fo' de Lawd, I b'lieves yo' would stay up dar wid dat boy an' ole mule till de Jedgment day, ef nobody called yo'."

Uncle Alex and the little boy came slowly to the house. The little boy said, " Aunt Rachel, the mule kicked Uncle Alex and broke the saddle." " Well I's glad uv it, honey. Dat ol' nigger f'ever'n' ter-nally foolin' 'roun' dat stable an' dat mule. Some-body bleege ter look atter 'im des same as de look atter yo' an' mo' so, fur dat matter, an' I aint er gwine ter do hit if de mule kill 'im. Eat yo' dinner, nigger, an' don' set dar an' look at me. Ef somebody bleeged ter watch yo' an' dat mule, dar neber would be nuthin' dun at dis house."

26

Alex ate his dinner in silence, for silence, he had learned by experience, was the best way to deal with Aunt Rachel. After dinner we went back to the stable, and saw the old mule lying down under the apple tree, and when we went to him, you can imagine our astonishment at finding him stone dead. Uncle Alex said, " Dar now, honey, dat mule dun busted his biler de same time he busted de saddle. Yo' know widout me tellin' yo' dat a mule can't fool wid Uncle Alex an' not git hurt." This was the last of our U. S. mule. Just what killed him we were never able to say.

This old negro lived with the Wiley family forty years. He had helped to nurse and rear and tell stories to the children and grandchildren of this family. His last act in life was to obey an order of his young mistress.

At his funeral I learned the following facts:

" Alex had been complaining only a few days. On the day of his death he sat in the kitchen, and Mrs. Jarman said to him, ' Uncle Alex, you had better go to your room and lie down, and I will bring you some gelatin.' He went to his room, and in a very short time Mrs. Jarman went to the door with the gelatin, and found the door locked. She said, ' Uncle Alex, open the door.' He did not reply. She repeated the order, ' Uncle Alex, open the door at once! ' He was sitting in a chair before the fire; he struggled to his feet, opened the door, went back and laid down on the bed, and in a moment was dead."

So passed from earth one of the most faithful men of his race, loved and respected by three generations of children, and white people. His last act was to obey his white mistress. Her last act concerning him was to minister to him in his sickness—a beautiful illustration of the faithful old slaves, and the love and respect they had for the Southern white people.

There is no " race question," if one is not made by politicians and people who know nothing of the conditions of the colored race, and his relation to the Southern white people. The race question will solve itself if let alone, and left to the two races that know and understand each other.

UNCLE PHIL'S VISIT TO HEAVEN

NCLE PHIL was a unique character, and yet you find a similar one in almost every community where there are many negroes. It would be difficult to make a pen picture of him, although his face and form are as clearly delineated now in my mind as on the day I last saw him; and the day I heard him tell of his trip to Heaven happened to be that day.

It was a singular fact—indeed, almost a coincidence—that the old negro died so shortly after telling the marvellous story of his visit to Heaven. I have no recollection of ever seeing him alive afterwards. He was found dead in a hay loft. He had evidently died in peace, sleeping quietly on the new-mown clover hay.

The hay loft was a favorite place for Uncle Phil to sleep, and he was permitted to do so at his pleasure. Being old, and not a very strong negro, and a favorite with the "white folks," he was not required to do much hard work. He generally looked after the horses, and took them to the blacksmith's shop, mended the harness, fed the chickens, found the turkey's nests, set the turkey hens, and helped them to take care of their broods.

He was great on killing rats, and could tell famous stories to the children about them, and about all sorts of animals, most of which were purely imaginary. You could hear him singing and praying at almost any hour, day or night, when about the stable. All the animals about the place knew Phil as well as the children knew him.

He was a religious fanatic, and yet he had no idea of what real religion consisted. He was never known to refuse either whiskey or tobacco when offered him, and yet, he was never known to be drunk. His master would say, "Phil, don't you know it is wrong for a Christian to drink whiskey?" He would reply:

"Yes, marster, but de Bible says, 'ligion never wuz zined to meck our pleasures less." According to Uncle Phil's moral code, it was right to do whatever he liked to do.

One evening after sun-down, when he came in for his supper, he leaned back in his split-bottomed chair, against the old locust tree that stood in the back yard, lit his pipe, and began to smoke and sing.

He had on a pair of tow linen trousers, with one suspender fastened to a button behind and to a wooden peg stuck through the trousers for a button in front; his cotton shirt was unbuttoned; he had on an old linen duster for a coat, an old black slouch hat on his head, a pair of old shoes on his feet, turned in at the heel and his toes sticking out, and a scant, kinky, snow-white beard on his face.

Aunt Rachel was the only one about the place that did not really love old Phil. She would say:

" I jest natully spises dat triflin' ole nigger—he allers pears to be so busy, an' he ain't do'en nuthin' on dis yer place sence he bin yere, cepin' walk roun' an' let on leck he so much ter do he dun know wat ter do fust. Dat's a 'ceitful ole nigger, an' if Miss Lizzie specs me fur ter feed an' cook fur dat ole nigger all de time, she is gwine ter be diserpinted, dat she is. Ef dey wuz ter let Rachel have her way, I boun yo' dey wouldn't have no po' ole, triflin', sneakin' creatur lak dat 'bout yere. Yo' cain't have any peace er mine fer seein' dat ole cripple nigger roun'—leastwise, he mek out he cripple, an' dar ain't no mo' de marter wid him dan dar is wid me, cep he wanter mek out to de white folks dat dar is. I hopes Mars John will give dat nigger erway to de fust nigger-trader dat comes by dis way."

It is difficult to say just how long Aunt Rachel would have continued this tirade, had she not been called in to attend to her duties in the house. It made very little impression, however, on Uncle Phil. But as the other darkies began to come in from about the place, and sit around talking while waiting for Aunt Rachel to give them supper, Uncle Andy said:

" Dis yere has been a powerful hot day—hit jes natully biles de grease outen a nigger. Dis ebnin' late, atter de sun dun drapped behine de hill, I yeard de birds chatterin' up in de woods, an' it peared ter me lek yo' could mighten nigh understand wat dey said. I heard one say, ' Bin ter ebbin! bin ter ebbin! bin ter ebbin! '—leastwise dats wat e sound lek e say." (This is a peculiar note of the wood-wren.)

Uncle Phil, upon hearing this, straightened himself up in his chair and said:

" Dat wood wren ain't de onliest one whar bin ter hebbin from dis place. I is dun bin dar myself."

" When is yo' bin dar, Unk Phil? " said Andy. " Ef yo' is dun bin dar, hits er God's pity yo' never staid dar, fur dat's de onliest time yo' is eber gwine ter git dar. How in de name er de Lawd duz it happen yo' dun cum back? "

" Well," said Phil, " I wuz out in de cone patch, behine de stable dis mawnin', er ploughin' dat roasin' year patch, en I wuz prayin' an' er prayin', when all at once I feel myself gin ter git light, an' I kep on er prayin' an' I git lighter an' lighter. After while I give er spring, an' I riz about as high as the cone tops. Then I come down an' prayed some mo', an' I felt myself gittin' light ergin, an' I jumped up, an' dis time I riz as high as de top er de fence; den I come down ergin; but I prayed some mo', an' I git light ergin; den I jumped up in de ar once mo' an', bless

32

"'I is dun bin dar myself.'"

Gaud, dis time de clouds tuck me; an' I went to de do' and knock, an' de Lawd say, ' Who dar ? ' And I say, ' Phillip, Lawd.' And de Lawd say, ' Go 'way from dar, Phillip; I don't know yo'.' Den I come on back down ter de cone patch, en I prays ergin; an' I gin ter git light, an' de fust time I jumped up de clouds tuck me. I go to de do' an' knock, an' de Lawd say, ' Who's dar ? ' an' I spon', ' Phillip, Lawd,' an' de Lawd said, ' Go roun' ter de back do'; ' an' I goes round an' knock, an' some one say, ' Who dar ? ' an' I spon', ' Phillip ! ' an' dey cum an' open de do' a leetle crack, an' I peeped in, an' no sich sights hab ebber fell on dis nigger's eyes befo'.

Dar they wuz, all settin' roun' de table eatin' sweet taters, an' watermillions, an' pumpkin pies, an' dey had coffee wid sweetnin' in it, an' dey wuz joyin' deyselfs monstrous; an' dar wuz one cheer dat dar ain't no one settin' in, an' de angel what open de do' say, ' Phillip, yo' see dat cheer wat empty ? ' I spon', ' I do.' Den he say, ' Dat's yo' seat wen yo' comes ter stay; but dey ain't no seat fer yo' ter-day.' Wid dat de cloud drapped me back in de cone patch, an' yere I is er waitin' fur dat empty cheer."

Aunt Rachel, who had come to call them to supper, heard the latter part of Phil's story, and she said, " Yes, ef yo' waits till yo' gits dat seat, watermillions will grow in de groun, an' sweet taters on de vine, an' pumpkin pies dun turn ter green simmons."

33

It was but three days after this, when the little boy went to the barn and climbed up in the loft that was nearly full of sweet, new clover hay (for it was haying season), and there lay Uncle Phil, apparently fast asleep, dressed in the old duster and tow linen trousers, just as he was the evening he told his story. The little boy pulled his coat and called to him, but he got no response. Then he shook him by the shoulder, but still no reply. He then called to Uncle Andy, who was nearby, to come and wake Uncle Phil. Uncle Andy said, " go way fum here, Honey, I aint got no time ter befoolin' wid ole Phil." The little boy insisted, and finally he came, and found poor old Phil had gone to claim the vacant chair.

UNCLE FRED AND THE YELLOW JACKETS

I T had been a long, hot day in July. The sun had literally " scotched the yearth," as Uncle Fred said. It was one of those days when everything looked like it wanted a drink of cool water. The corn blades were twisted, and the grass looked dry and parched. The cattle sought the shade of the trees or waded in the creeks to get relief from the heat.

We were in the cornfield ploughing corn, going over it for the last time that season—" laying it by," the negroes called it. Fred had done a hard day's work, ploughing with an old, long-legged, blazed-faced sorrel horse that " Mars Willum," as the darkies called him, had ridden home one day from the army.

.I remember well the day he came home, and the day he left. He rode away on " Pat," an iron-gray mare of fine blood and good speed, and as game as a horse could be. He left the old sorrel in her place —his name was Sam.

Now Sam was as vexatious a horse as any sorrel horse could possibly be. In those day I thought the color of a horse had lots to do with his disposition, and to this day I am of the belief that there are more mean sorrel horses than of any other color. Sam had given Uncle Fred a great deal of trouble that day; he seemed to take special pleasure in being " cantankerous." The truth is, if Fred had been a horse he would have been a sorrel himself, for he was a high-tempered, long-legged, raw-boned negro, as " black as the ace of spades," and as mean as any sorrel horse that ever lived—a fact which Sam (the horse) had very soon found out; so that between the negro and the horse there was a mutual hatred, as strong as ever existed between a cat and a dog.

Sam had worried Uncle Fred that day all he could, and by evening Fred was, as usual, in his very worst frame of mind, and old Sam, with his long, winding legs and sore back, was a picture of misery; for no matter how much you fed him, or how well you cared for him, he would never get any fatter, and Fred was built on the same pattern: He could eat more than any living man, and it apparently had as little effect on him as corn had on Sam.

About three o'clock on this hot July evening Fred had ploughed out to the end of the row, and stopped to shade a few moments and " let Sam blow," as he called it. Now, there is one thing on a hot July day that is as busy as on any other day—Fred said busier —and that is yellow jackets. Fred calls them " yaller jackets."

"Fred was sitting on the plow handle nodding."

A " yaller jacket " is a kind of wasp, somewhat smaller than a honey bee, and gets its name from the yellow stripes around its body. They make their nest in the ground, and when disturbed swarm out by the hundreds, and woe to the one that stirs up a " yaller jacket's nest," for they can sting faster and harder and more times to the minute than any other insect in the world.

While Sam was blowing and Fred was sitting on the plough handle, with the plough lines around his wrist, nodding, it occurred to the little boy to devise a plan to wake Fred up suddenly and surely.

He had a large, shaggy Newfoundland dog that followed him everywhere he went, and would do almost anything he wanted her to do. She would carry a package or go after a ball, stick, or other object thrown to any distance, and bring it back to you. Hard by, under the root of an old stump, was a big nest of yellow jackets. The little boy knew that if he threw a stick near the nest the yellow jackets would swarm out, and that when the dog went to fetch the stick they would swarm about her and follow her as she returned with the stick. He knew also that her coat was so shaggy that the yellow jackets could not sting her, but that, when she got as far as old Sam, and Fred nodding between the plough handles, they would try something on which their stingers would be more effective.

37

So the little boy called Juno, and threw his stick close to the nest of yellow jackets, and out they came by the hundreds, and when Juno ran up and got the stick the yellow jackets began swarming about her, and followed her as she ran back to the plough. When Juno got to the plough, the little boy being by this time a safe distance away, the yellow jackets at once turned their attention from Juno to Sam and Fred. Sam gave one plunge and took Fred backwards over the plough handles, dragging him and the plough through the cornfield, the dust and dirt flying like a small whirlwind. It was but a very short distance to the woods on that side of the cornfield, and Sam made for the bushes, taking the plough and Fred with him. There was a " brush pile " at the edge of the woods, and just there the plough lines broke, freeing Fred, and landing him about the middle of the brush heap, while Sam went on to the interior of the woods, leaving the plough hung to a sapling.

The joke had assumed a more serious turn than had been anticipated, and the little boy was terribly frightened at first, when he saw Sam taking Uncle Fred with him to the woods; he had not noticed that he had the plough lines around his wrist. However, no one knew what made Sam run away, except the little boy and Juno, and Juno could not talk; moreover, even if she had had the gift of speech she would have kept the little boy's secret.

Fortunately, Uncle Fred was not hurt; and when the little boy got to him, which he did as quickly as possible, the picture which Uncle Fred presented in the middle of the brush pile was one never to be effaced from his memory. Fred had not even made an effort to extricate himself. There he sat, his shirt and trousers hanging in shreds about him, and, strange to say, somehow the old, greasy slouch hat, that had some time in its history been been white, still stuck to his head with the brim flopped down. He was covered with dust from head to foot, and one old shoe gone. Of course, he had on no socks, for none of the negroes wore socks in the summer. The perspiration was pouring down his face, and had made paths through the dust on his cheeks. Uncle Fred, as already stated, was a tall, slim negro, with high cheek-bones, rather small eyes, and the only person, except one, that I ever saw, the white of whose eyes showed all the way around. He had a fine set of teeth as white as pearls and his skin as black as ebony, and the only real black negro I have ever seen with thin lips.

There he sat, too full for utterance. When the little boy got to him he said, " Uncle Fred, are you hurt ? " It was some moments before he replied. Then he rolled his little black eyes and said:

39

" Is yo' hurt? is yo' hurt? Dat's er putty question fer ter be axin', when yo' done seed dat d——
ole sor'l Yankee hoss, whar Mars Willum done fotch
year, done drug me wid dem plough lines clean up in
dis woods, an' lef' me er settin' in de middle of dis
year bresh heap, an' yo' kin go to de house an' tell
Rachel dis is de Lawd's trufe. Dat I is done dead an'
berried in dis year bresh pile, an' dat ole Yankee
hoss what Mars Willum done fetch year is de very
man what done hit. An' wen I gits outen yer, I's
er gwine meck dat hoss wush he ain't neber seed no
bresh pile. He done stood dar twell he think Fred
wuz er sleep, an' den up and tuck and run off. I'll
let 'em know Fred's not ersleep eve'r time 'e got 'es
eyes shot, yo' year."

With this Uncle Fred proceeded to crawl out of the
brush heap.

The little boy did not dare to tell Uncle Fred for a
year afterwards what made " Ole Sam " run away.

THE CORN SHUCKING

I T was not uncommon in the days gone by for the farmers in the community to have what they called " a corn shucking " in the Fall of the year. After the corn was ripe and ready for shucking (husking) it was pulled from the stalks with the shucks (husks) on, and loaded into wagons and hauled to a place convenient to the barn or corn cribs, and piled into two piles aimed to be of equal size. Word was then sent to all the neighbors round about, that there would be a corn shucking at this place on a certain night. Of course, these corn shuckings always came off during the light of the moon.

Moonlight nights in the South, especially during the Fall of the year, are beautiful almost beyond description. In fact, I have never seen a description of a typical moonlight night during the month of October that even approached an adequate portrayal of its real beauty. Indeed, it cannot be delineated by a pen picture, neither can it be represented by a real picture. There is something about the soft beauty of the Southern moonlight, the pure freshness of the air, and the lights and shadows of the trees, hills, and mountains, that no combination of colors

41

spread by the most skilful artist can reproduce. It is of matchless beauty and loveliness.

The object of a corn-shucking is that the owner of the corn may get it all shucked out in a single night by the aid of his neighbors' hands, and he is therefore expected, as a remuneration for their services, to make it a festive occasion. After the shucking is over a big supper is served, and a prize given to the captain of the gang who gets his pile of corn shucked first. Before the shucking begins, and while the crowd is assembling, those who come early spend the time sitting around telling jokes and walking about sizing up the two piles of corn. After they have all assembled, two are chosen from the crowd for captains. After this is done, the captains choose their men. The first choice is decided by one captain spitting on a chip and throwing it up in the air, and saying to the other captain, "Wet or dry?" If the side named by the latter is up he gets first choice; if otherwise, his opponent has first choice. After the sides are chosen they again toss the chip for choice of corn piles. This all being arranged, each captain makes his speech, after which the work begins. It was looked upon as a great honor among the negroes at that time to be selected "captain" at a corn shucking. There would be as much wire-pulling for this honor as there is among the politicians of to-day for the nomination to Congress. They showed great skill in this, too, and often more honesty than the latter-day politician.

On this particular occasion Uncle Andy Campbell (named after General Campbell, of Kings Mountain fame) was chosen captain of the one crowd, and Lace Fullen of the other. Both of these negroes were as " black as the ace of spades," but as entirely different in appearance as in mental qualities. They were both unique characters and highly respected by the " white folks," as well as by the negroes. In " negro quarters " Uncle Andy was authority, and Lace Fullen " de law and Gospel." Andy was a tall, slender man of quick movement, active as a cat, and it was considered a great feat to throw Andy in a wrestling match. Lace was of the opposite build. He was short, heavy set, slow of motion, and the negroes said, " The only difference 'tween Unk' Lace an a hoss wuz, dat de hoss want quite ez strong ez Lace."

A great many of the white people were in attendance on these occasions to enjoy the songs and dances. They always had a place fixed for dancing, either on boards, or a flat, smooth place on the ground; and old Joe, the famous " banjo picker," was always present.

I wish I could accurately reproduce the speeches of these two men as I heard them that night, but my memory is somewhat at fault. It is, by the way, rather remarkable that although it has been many

years since these corn shuckings were in vogue, there
has never appeared in print, as far as I know, any
attempt to reproduce one of these speeches.

Uncle Andy won on both tosses of the chip, and
he was considered to be in great luck at the outset.
Aunt Rachel said, " Dat nigger allers wuz lucky
frum de day he wuz borned. He ain't neber seed no
hard times yit, even wen the Yankees wuz yer; he
staid right whar he is now, and tain't nobuddy bod-
der 'im."   Uncle Andy said, " He wouldn't give de
en' er Mars Sam's big toe fer all de Yankees in de
wurl."   At this point Aunt Rachel's speech was cut
short by Andy saying:

" Go ter de house, Rachel, and tend ter gittin' dat
supper, kaze dese niggers will be dar fur it fo' yo'
has time to roas' dem sweet taters, an' bake dem
pumpkin pies—mor'n dat, I's got sumpin myself to
say to dese niggers. Now yo' fling yo' eye over dis
cone pile, and fling yo' eye on dat yuther cone pile,
an' den fling yo' eye on dat yuther crowd er niggers,
an' yo' see wat yo' got ter do. Yo' sees dat I dun
tuck de biggest pile er cone an' I dun choose de weakliest crowd er men. I do dat kaze I knows Lace is
gwine ter say, I dun tuck de littlest pile er cone an'
de biggest men, an' fur dat reason we don beat 'em;
kaze yo' know Lace en his crowd done beat now.
Didn't I say sumpin' den ? " " Yes, yo' sed sumpin' "
(from the crowd).   " Tooby, sho' I sed sumpin, an'

44

Lace knows hit. Lace knows a mud turkle can't ketch a rabbit, any mor'n he kin ketch Andy. Wen yo' pick up a yere er cone, I want yer to do hit dis way" (here Andy took an ear of corn and ran it through his hand, and it was husked as quickly as if done by machinery). "See, dat's de way ter shuck cone! Now, I ain't got no mo' ter say. Yo' know de lick wat its done by, an' I's done show dem de lick, an' wen we is done beat 'em, tain't no use ter say 'Andy is done cheated.' De nigger whar say dat is a liar, an' de truf ain't in 'im. An' if it wuz, wat yer gwine ter do 'bout it? I can fling any nigger down wat dars ter try me, atter dis yere shuckin' is ober —an 'ef yo's got anything ter say, now's the time ter say it. De cone breads er bakin', the sweet taters roasin', de ole hams er bilin', de chickens er stewin', de coffee is er steamin' in de pot, an' dat ole 'Apple Jack' wat Mars Sam is got, is jes natully bustin' the cork."

"Shet yo' mouf!" (from the crowd).

"Yes, honey, shet yo' mouf on some er dat pumkin pie, wen dis yer cone is shucked—dat's de time ter shet yo' mouf, an 'open yo' mouf, too."

"I's gittin' hungry now!" (from the crowd).

"A hungry nigger is wuth two niggers wid dey bellies full."

It is difficult to tell how long this talk would have gone on had not Lace interrupted it by saying:

45

" Hit jes meck a man hungry to look at dat long slick, black po' nigger, let er lone yearin' 'im stand dar en talk 'bout dem ar things ter eat. I jes' ain't er gwine ter stand it no longer; it's time dis shuckin' dun begin; an' fur dat matter, it's time it wuz dun. But Andy said he tuck de littlest pile er cone an' de weakliest men, kaze he don't want Lace ter say dar wuz cheatin'. Dat nigger ez jis' wat he looks lack— a black snake. He blacker an' slicker dan er snake; an' he dun try to 'ceive yo' niggers by sayin' he tuck de littlest pile er cone an' de weakliest men, wen he dun got de pick er bofe. But dat ain't no 'count; Lace ain't gon' no whar yit; mor'n dat, Andy dun 'pared hisself ter er rabbit, an' me ter er mud turkle. He dun fergit how de turkle dun wun de race frum de rabbit; but Lace'll call hit ter his membrance befo' he dun wid dis yere cone shuckin'."

" Dat's hit! " (from the crowd).

" Tooby sho' dat's hit, an' Lace gwine ter show yo' dat's hit; er furdermo', Andy dun said he kin fling any nigger downs wats at dis shuckin'. Andy kin fling some niggers, dat's de trufe; but yere's er nigger back whar Andy can't touch de groun' wid. Yo 'seed Andy shuck dat year cone jes' dis way " (here Lace picked up an ear of corn and shucked it just as Andy had done) " an' he think nobody kin do dat but 'im. But I boun', wen dat ar pile er cone is dun, dis yere one dun bin dun er half hour, an' our

46

han's and face dun wash fer supper; an' dat Apple
Jack dun bus' outen de bottle fo' he gits dar; an'
Aunt Rachel's sweet taters half col'; an' de coffee-
pot bile over; an' de pumkin pie gown down de red
lane; an' ol' Drum dun got de ham bone an' gone
wid it."

By this time the negroes were worked up to the
highest tension.

The shucking began at nine o'clock; by twelve
" Uncle Lace's " men raised a shout; they had tossed
the last ear in; not a nubbin was left. This was a
great back-set to Uncle Andy, especially since he had
the choice of the corn piles and the first pick of the
men. Andy was not a negro to be easily defeated
at a corn shucking, and it was not quite understood
why, with fortune favoring him, Lace should have
been the victor, for it was full thirty minutes before
Andy's pile was finished. It was not difficult to see
that Andy felt his defeat very keenly, and Lace was
by no means modest enough not to gloat over his vic-
tory. He said:

" I dun tole yo' fo' yo' begin, I be dun half hour
fo 'yo'; en dar yo' is er shuckin' er way, same ez ef
yo' des commenced. Yo' wasin' yo' time er foolin'
wid Lace en his men. De next time yo' needn't be
so peart 'bout sayin', ' Dis is de way to shuck cone.'
We don sho' yo' de way, en we kin sho' de way to
do yuther things sides dat. Yo' dun said yo' kin fling

any nigger down whar is at dis shuckin'. I's er nigger whar yo' can't fling; an' mo'n dat, ain't nary yuther nigger yere whar kin do it."

This was more than Andy could stand, for he was already smarting under defeat; but he took no risks, for he was very shrewd, and knew well enough that, if Lace once got him in his grasp he could not resist his great strength; whereas, Andy's forte was in his activity and skill as a wrestler. He never intended to give Lace a chance to get his arms around him. So he said:

" Tooby sho', yo' dun beat us er shuckin'; tooby sho' yo' is, kaze three er my bes' men dun cut der fingers no sooner den dey begin shuckin', en yo' niggers dun put pounded glass in de cone; kaze I dun foun' de glass whar wuz in dar, an' if I know de nigger wha put it en dar, Andy kin whoop 'im, en dar ain't no pounded glass whar kin help 'im. Yo' kin talk mighty proud, an' yo' kin talk mighty loud, but dat's all yo' kin do. Ef yo' wants ter fling Andy, why don't yo' dres yo'self to dat pint."

At this Lace made a rush like a mad bull for Andy, but he was expecting this, and had been doing everything he could to provoke Lace to make the attack. So as quick as a flash he dropped to the ground and met Lace's rush by catching him just about the knees, throwing him as clear over his head as if he had been but a ten-year-old boy, and landing in the middle of the pile of corn shucks, amid the shouts and laughter of the crowd.

"Go it, Unc' Andy! We knowed Lace ain't er gwine ter do nothin' wid yo'."

"No, chillen, he ain't er gwine ter do nuthin' wid me. I des 'lowed dem ter shuck de cone fust to keep der diserpintment from bein' too 'stressin'. I dun berried dat nigger in dem cone shucks, ter look fur de glass dey put in dar."

By this time Lace had crawled out and was making his preparations for another rush, but this time with more caution; for "two falls out of three" lost the wrestling match. Lace said, "Yo is er feared ter try me wid fair holts."

Andy replied, "Wat yo' call fair holts? Does yo' think I's gwine ter come up en lay down in yo' arms? Dat's lek de frog in de huckleberry patch—des let de black snake swaller 'em fo' 'e does his kickin'; den wen 'e kick, dey ain't no groun' under 'e foot, en 'e keint git no foot-hol', so dar 'e is; but I gwine ter do my kickin' fust."

"Tooby sho' yo' is; tooby sho' yo' is," said Lace; "but ef I gits my paw on yo', yo' do yo' las' kickin' fus', kaze at de las' yo' won't have no breff to kick wid."

With this Lace made a second rush for Andy, but Andy dodged, and before he could turn caught him by the foot, and threw him flat on his back on the

49

smooth, hard ground which they had prepared for the dancing. The fall was a clear one and a hard one. So Andy was the winner, and his crowd raised a wild yell, for they knew there was not another "nigger" at the shuckin' that could have dusted Lace's back. Andy said, "De black bar done cum er long en set 'e foot in Andy's trap, an' dar 'e is."

With this, old Joe began to pick the banjo and the dancing immediately began. A dance at a corn shucking cannot be reproduced on paper, nor can it be described; it belongs to the past, and can only be enjoyed as a memory by the Southern white people and others who may have chanced to witness it.

At about this juncture Aunt Rachel, with her red handkerchief on her head, appeared on the scene and said, "Wat yo' niggers er doin' out yere keepin' me er waitin' dat supper? Andy dun let Lace beat 'im shuckin' cone; and Lace dun 'lowed dat little slick black nigger to mighten nigh des natully bus' de groun' open wid 'im; an' yer de coffee, an' de hot biskits, an' de fried chicken, and de sweet taters ("Shet yo' mouf!" from the crowd) is er all gittin' col'; an' moe'n dat, I's got dem dishes ter wash atter yo' niggers is dun had yo' supper; en 'sides dat Marse Sam dun moved de stopper from de jug."

No further invitation was needed. There was but one thing a negro loved better at a corn shucking than dancing, and that was eating; so without further urging on Aunt Rachel's part they went to the kitchen and enjoyed eating and drinking as only negroes could.

What would many a millionaire give for the health and digestion of one of those plantation negroes? And yet, we are told in such books as " Uncle Tom's Cabin," and by other writers of that type, who knew almost nothing of slave life in the South, of the dreary, hopeless life they led, knowing nothing but the hardest work, driven by the master's lash, without one ray of sunshine or pleasure. I honestly believe as a race, slaves on the Southern plantations were the happiest, best-contented people the sun ever shone on.

THE SNAKE CHARMER

I T was on the 21st of July, 18—, as hot a day as I have ever known. The sun had reached its zenith and seemed to stand still. The whole world seemed still; not a twig or leaf was moving. The grain fields looked like seas of gold, with not a ripple on the surface. There was not an animal in sight on the old plantation; they had all sought the shade of the wood; the birds had disappeared to some shady spot; the insects had ceased their hum, except the jar-flies' discordant note from a nearby tree, and now and then the droning of a drowsy beetle.

It was one of those " copper days," when the shimmer of the heat had a peculiar sort of metallic lustre, and when the least exertion brought exhaustion.

I had stretched myself on the ground in the shade of a spreading oak, to wait for the world to waken up, and had fallen asleep. Suddenly I was startled by the most unearthly scream I'd ever heard. I sprang from the ground at a bound, with my heart beating like a drum. I looked hastily about me, but saw no one; everything seemed as quiet and peaceful as before. I sat down and tried to think whether I had

been dreaming, or whether I had really heard a ter-
rific scream. Again I looked in every direction, but
there was no one in sight. I sat down again, and was
saying aloud to myself, "That certainly was strange,"
when a wild laugh came from the tree over my head
and startled me again. I looked up and saw, sitting
among the branches of the tree, a most remarkable
and singular person, known in the community as
" Nipper, the snake charmer." I knew Nipper to be
a harmless fellow, but he had certainly given me a
fright. I told him to come down, which he did as
quickly as a cat, and seated himself on the ground in
front of me. The first thing he said was, " Give me
a chaw er terbacker." I complied with his request.

Nipper was a small man, his skin about the color
of smoked bacon. He had one of those smooth, sal-
low skins, on which beard does not grow. His eyes
were bright blue, his hair light and thin, his chin
small, and lips rather thick. He had neither eye-
brows nor lashes; had a deep, smooth, pleasant voice,
but spoke with a drawl, and was an incessant talker.
He had on a blue cotton shirt, fastened with one button at the collar; and a pair of trousers that had once
been light in color. These were held up by one leather
suspender. His feet were without shoes. Altogether
he was not a very attractive specimen to be called a
" charmer," and yet there was that about his voice
that was very attractive and pleasant. After seeing

" A wild laugh came from the tree over my head."

him it was always hard to realize that such a voice belonged to Nipper.

On account of his eccentric ways, and the fact that he generally had a snake concealed about his person, most people avoided him. The negroes had an absolute dread of him. They believed he was in league with Satan, and that he had the power to put "squaw-pins" (scorpions) in you. All animals were fond of him, and he had great control over them. I said:

" Nipper, what were you doing up in that tree? You nearly scared me out of my wits. Why did you scream that way? "

" Wal, now ter tell the truf, I been er bout this tree fer mighty nigh two days, er tryin' ter ketch er snake wat stays about yer. Hit air the only snake ever I seed that I couldn't ketch; en when you cum and laid down thar he run off, en if it hadn't been fer you I would er kotch him, en when I seed you wuz asleep, I jist up en hollered ter skeer yer, an' by Gosh! I cum putty nigh doin' it."

I asked him what sort of a snake it was.

" It wur a black snake. There air some bird nest in this yer tree, en he cums yer to git the eggs, en I 'lowed if I got up in the tree fust I could nab him wen he cum up."

I asked, " What were you going to do with him if you had got him? "

" I wuz goin' ter take him home ter ketch rats.

Black snakes is powerful fond er rats, and one black snake kin ketch more rats in er day than two cats kin ketch in er week."

" Well, ain't you afraid of snakes about the house ? " I asked.

" Lawd, no; I ain't no more feared uv snakes than I am uv a rat."

" Don't they ever bite you ? "

" I've been bit nineteen times; but I don't mind ther bites; hit don't hurt much nohow. I kin cure snake bites. But one bit me tother day that hurt me wuss than any one yit. I hed er big rattlesnake in er box at the house, en one er my boys had been whoopin' it with switches to make it mad. When I cum in, I tuck it outen the box ter play with. I didn't know the boys had been er whoopin' it, en when I hed hit up close to my face I looked away fer sumpin, en hit popped me right between the eyes. Don't you see them little red spots ther now ? I foun' out one thing: if anybody is bin pesterin' er rattlesnake, en specially er whoopin' it with switches, they is mighty apt ter bite yer, ef yer don't handle em powerful keerful. Snakes will bite yer anyhow ef yer ain't keerful, kaze I hed er man the yuther day er helpin' me cleer off some new ground, en ther wuz er lot uv bresh on the place. The man wuz mighty keerless 'bout ther way he handled ther bresh. So I said, ' Look yere, er copperhead will bite you terectly ef

56

yo' ain't more keerful.' And he said, 'Nipper, I ain't feared no snakes. I'm in ther hands er ther Lord, en ther Lord won't suffer er snake ter bite me. I am er member uv ther church, I serve ther Lord, en He won't 'low no snake ter bite me.' I said, ' Look yere, I hev bin er follin' with snakes fer er long time, and ther is one thing sho', ther Lord don't extend His business ez fer ez copperhead snakes.' En hit wasn't ten minutes till ther biggest kin' er one hung him in ther back er ther hand, en I swar yer could er heard 'im holler er mile. I said, ' Look er yer, hev you en ther Lord done zolved partnership er ready ? I tole yer there Lord didn't extend His business ez fer ez copperheads.' En if I hadn't put some er my snake medicine on ther bite hit would er mighty nigh kilt him."

About this time there was a little motion about the front of Nipper's shirt, and a big black snake poked his head out, and licked out his tongue in a threatening way. I did not need any invitation to change my seat.

" Nipper, there is a big snake in your shirt," I said.

" Wal, yer know, I carries that one ter hunt squirrels with when I go er huntin', and if ther squirrels go in er hole, this yer snake will run em out. I kin kill more squirrels in er day than any yuther man in these mountains. Jes take 'im in yer han's an' let 'im run down yer shirt collar, an' see how slick 'e is."

With this he started towards me.

" Sit down, Nipper; don't come any nearer. I don't like snakes as well as you do."

He grinned a broad grin, took his seat, and the snake disappeared in his shirt.

This eccentric man had gotten the name of " snake charmer," not only because he caught and handled snakes, but because, for some strange reason, snakes, as well as all other animals, loved him. He could go and sit down alone, and by some peculiar sound could call snakes from their hiding places, and you could see them stick their heads up out of the grass near him. He disclaimed knowing any reason for his power over snakes, other than that he was not " afeared uv 'em, en they knew it."

The one other singular thing about him was the marvellous softness and sweetness and attractiveness of his voice. You could listen to him talk for hours and not feel tired. There was something soothing in the sound of his voice. The negroes said it was the Devil.

While we were engaged in this conversation, Uncle Andy and the Little Boy came up. The Little Boy knew Nipper and liked him, but Andy had a great aversion to him, and said, " Come er long, honey; we ain't got no time ter be foolin' long with Marse Sam, en mo' en dat, Miss Lizzie done said fer us ter hurry back."

"But Uncle Andy, I want to hear Nipper talk a while and tell me about the way he catches snakes."

"Nuver min' about Mr. Nipper's snakes. I spec' he done got some in he' pocket now, an' de fus' thing you know he done bite yo'. Dat's a dangous white pusson ter spen' yo' time wid, honey. Dar ain't nobody whar kin tote snakes in der pocket but what is dangous."

About this time the black snake stuck his head out of Nipper's shirt again. Uncle Andy said, "Fo' God, honey, I ain't er gwine ter stay narry nuther minit. Don't yo' see dat snake?" And he seized the Little Boy by the hand and started off in a trot, saying, "Yo' kin charm snakes if yer want ter, but yer not er gwine ter charm Andy with yer sof' voice and yer ragged close. Yo' ain't nuthin' but de Debil nohow, en Mars Sam is er foolin' his time er way talkin' wid yo'."

The Little Boy said, "Uncle Andy, do you really think Nipper would hurt anybody?"

"Not ef yo' is er watchin' 'im; but 'e kin put er spell on yer, en nobody kin mobe hit but Witch Mary, en she done daid en gone. En Nipper gwine ter jine her some er dese days, kaze dey is one en de same sort er pussons. En whar one goes wen dey dies, de yuther gwine ter go, too; and I dunno wat kin' er place it gwine ter be, nuther. I wish Nipper was dar right now wid his snakes!"

" But, Uncle Andy, Witch Mary went to Heaven, because she told us she was going; and that the children would bring flowers and put them over her body when she died, and everybody says they did."

" Yes, honey, but nobody knows whar dem flowers cum frum; en 'sides date, some folks say dem flowers was scotched—leastways, dey say dey smell like dey wuz scotched. Yo' kin put no 'pendence on whar Mary is, or whar Nipper is gwine. But one thing sho', he ain't er gwine ter cum close to Andy. I ain't neber struck no white man yit, but ef Nipper wuz ter git me in a close place, en 'proach me wid dem snakes, I would be 'bleeged ter let 'im feel de weight er dis yere black paw! "

Nipper is still living; but Uncle Andy has long since passed away, and, strange to say, he died from the effects of a snake bite.

HOW THE LITTLE BOY GOT FRIGHTENED
AT THE CANDLE MOULDS

T was a cold, dark night; the wind was blowing a fierce gale, the sleet was rattling against the window-panes, and the shutters were creaking on their hinges. The children were around a big, blazing wood fire in an old-fashioned fire-place, roasting Irish potatoes in the ashes, and popping corn. Mother was sitting in the corner making a cap for one of the boys, and Aunt Rachel was sitting in the other corner knitting.

One of the children said, " Aunt Rachel, tell us a tale."

Aunt Rachel had a red bandanna handkerchief tied around her head, and a red striped linsy dress on, and was the picture of an old-time black mammy. I can see her in my mind's eye as clearly as if she stood before me this minute; her delight was to tell stories to the children after candle light. During the war we always burned candles, which were moulded out of beef-tallow. The moulds when not in use stood on a shelf in the store-room. We had just asked Aunt Rachel to tell us a tale, and, although she was very fond of telling us stories, she was never known in all

61

her life to begin one on such occasions except under protest.

"Now yo' chillens knows I's not er gwine to tell no tale ter night; so yo' just as well let ole Rachel 'lone. Mo'ne dat, even if I wuz gwine ter tell yo' a tale, I done know no tale ter tell; so yo' mout jis as well roas' dem taters and pop dat co'n and let Rachel 'lone kaze she not er gwine ter tell no tale dis night."

Now this was the signal that Rachel would in a very few moments be spinning us a yarn, and we were respectfully quiet, and went on with our corn popping, as sure that the tale would be forthcoming as that we were alive. After awhile Aunt Rachel "sorter" straightened herself up and said:

"I do declar, I's gittin' so no-'count I can't see to knit by dese candles. I draps a stitch eber minit might'n nigh, and can't no mo' pick it up en er owl kin see in de day time. Is eber I done tole yo' chillen bout dat owl I seed once wat could talk?"

"No, Aunt Rachel; tell us about it."

"Well, hits a curious thing 'bout dat owl. I dun mos' fegit how hit wuz myself, but I know one thing: dat owl could talk mos' es good es yo' kin; and mo'en dat, he knowed wat he talken 'bout. I was er gwine 'long out yander one day todes dem woods whar dat man was berried de fus year er de war, wat dey say done died wid de yaller janders, and de fus thing I knowed I yerd some one say, 'Who-whoo: who-whoo:

62

" ' Who dat say who-whoo ? ' "

who air yer—who-whoo, who-whoo—who air yer?'
An' I tuck and stop, I did, an' lissen, en I nebber yerd
nothin' more; and den I move 'long agin, sorter slow,
kaze I don' leck de soun' ob dat voice, kaze I yerd
sum folks say dat de man whar died wid de yaller
janders hed bin seed fo' now, walkin' 'bout dem
woods, an' I 'lowed hit mout be 'im, axen ' Who air
yer?' en ef hit wuz, I tell yo' now, chillens, Aunt
Rachel ain't got much time ter talk wid live folks,
en got no time 'tal ter talk wid ded uns. An' mo'en
dat, sum people says yaller janders is ketchin. So I
jis start out putty peart fur de house, when sumpin
said again, ' Who-whoo: who air yer?' an' so I
'lowed it wuz time fur Rachel to 'spond when anybody ax who air yer. So I up en' said, ' My name's
Rachel, en' I don keer ef hit is, en t'aint nun of
yo' bizness ef hits Rachel or not. I's er gwine er
long yere er tending to my bizness, en' I aint got no
time ter be foolin' long wid yo'.' So wid dat I up
and start home agin, en den sumpin' say, ' Who air
yer,' agin. Dis time hit soun' lek hit wuz rite in de
trees 'bove my hed, an' wen I looks up dar, wat does
I see but one dese great big whoppin' owls, wid
his eyes as big as de yaller of a egg, and shinin' jist
zactly lek a glass marvel. Den I knowed hit was
dis owl wat wuz er hollerin' at me, en I up en lowed
yo' had better git out dat tree, kaze we aint got no
chicken fur yo' bout dis place. An' wid dat he turn

63

he hed clean roun' over he shoulder and look at me, so straight, I clar to goodness, chillen, I feel sorter cu'ious, en dem eyes look so big en yaller dat I lit out and come home sailin'."

About this stage of the story, mother said, " Son, go out to the kitchen and tell Uncle Andy to bring some wood in for the fire." The little boy started out, and opened the door that went through the hall to the kitchen. The plastering was off the wall in one place, and the light from the blazing fire shone through the laths on the candle moulds, so that the reflection from the tin made them shine very bright, and to his youthful imagination, after hearing Aunt Rachel's owl story, made the candle moulds look like the great big owl eyes. He stood for one moment, and then rushed back into the room with one wild scream, " shiney eyes looking at me!! " Everybody rushed to the hall to see, and there were the candle-moulds standing in the store room and shining through the cracks in the wall, which he had taken for " Shiney eyes." When the commotion was settled, Aunt Rachel said, " well, I declar to de Laud, I is not er gwine ter tell yo' chillen no mo' tales uv nights; dis yer chile dun skeered me out'en my senses holler'n 'bout shiney eyes lookin' at 'im."

HOW THE LITTLE BOYS BROKE UP A REVIVAL

WHILE sitting here looking out of my window and watching some little boys play ball in the back lot of a store-building, I am carried back to my boyhood days, just after, and during the latter part of, the war between the North and South. I can remember many of the impressions made upon my youthful mind, and many of the incidents connected with those days. Then most of my time was spent playing with the little "niggers," and listening to the older ones tell their many queer stories, couched in their own peculiar language which I have here endeavored to reproduce just as it sounded to me then.

The negro dialect or folk-lore of the negro race, as we heard it in those days, is fast disappearing, and it is only among the older negroes that you hear the genuine negro dialect. The language of the younger generation of negroes, that have grown up since the war, is a strange conglomeration of negro talk and bad grammar, resulting in part from their tendency to imitate their white neighbors; so that it is positively refreshing to meet and hear an " old time " " old issue " negro talk.

In those days my nearest neighbor owned an old fat negro man of the name of Harvey King, who spent his time looking after the boys, to help keep them out of mischief. We always called him Uncle Harvey. Now Uncle Harvey was a character in his way, and was a good, religious old man, and spent many of his hours singing and praying I can almost hear now the old negro's voice singing his evening hymns, but cannot remember the words of his songs. Why this is so seems to me strange. When, however, I think over it carefully I am persuaded that he did not really use words. Nevertheless, his songs to me were beautiful, and I know the old man is now with the saints on the other shore:— In fact, he must have been almost a saint here to have borne patiently, as he did, the many pranks we boys played on him.

We spent a good part of our time doing things especially to worry and annoy Uncle Harvey; not that we did not love him, but because we did not want him with us all the time, and at other times we behaved provokingly just to hear him talk. But we were as loyal to Uncle Harvey as he was to us. No one would do anything unfriendly to him without stirring up a hornet's nest about his ears. No matter what the white boys did to annoy or tease him, it would have been dangerous for anyone else to attempt it. So the old man was as sure of our affection for him as we were of his for us. I do not remember that he ever reported any of us to our parents for anything we did, although he would constantly threaten to do so. How he managed to make us believe he would do so, when there was never an instance of his having done so, is a mystery. The two older boys were the hardest for him to manage and they led the old man a dance; but in the main, he was equal to all emergencies.

One evening, just after sundown, Uncle Harvey lost track of " the boys," and he said to the little boy, " Honey, does yo' know whar Willum and Sildum is ? " He replied, " Uncle Harvey, I heard them say they were going to Smyth's School-house to preaching." " Dun gone to Smif's School-house is dey ? Well, I is er gwine atter 'em rite now—does yo' want ter go, honey ? " The little boy replied that he did, so off they started.

Smyth's School-house was a log building located about a mile from our home, and was used both for a school and a church. The Methodist circuit-rider had a regular appointment to preach there once a month, and sometimes there would be a protracted meeting and an old-fashioned revival, where everybody in the community would profess religion, and would shout and sing, and shake hands and laugh and cry, all at the same time, and embrace each other, and renew their vows to "meet me in heaven."

It was to one of these revival meetings that the boys had gone, when Uncle Harvey missed them. Uncle Harvey was about as much pleased to go to the meetings as the boys, for all the white folks liked him, and he loved them; he knew how to "wait on de white folks," and he liked to do it. Freedom (emancipation) was no blessing to Uncle Harvey, for he had his white friends who supplied his every want, and the white children would divide anything they had with "Uncle Harvey." He knew his place, kept it, and was loved and respected by the white folks, till the day of his death, and his memory is still cherished by hundreds who knew him.

As we journeyed on our way to the old meeting-house, we came to a little patch of woods, through which the road passed, about the time it was getting dark. Uncle Harvey, like all of his race, was superstitious, and the shadows of evening always filled the old man's mind with weird fancies. It was his hour for inspiration, and well the children knew it. The Little Boy said, " Uncle Harvey, people say this place is haunted; do you believe it ? "

" Cose I believes it, honey; aint I dun seed hants 'bout yere fo' dis, but I's not feared er no hants, an' mo' 'en dat, honey, dis yer aint de time night fur

" ' Uncle Harvey, people say this place is haunted.' "

hants; hants don't truble fo' midnight. Aint yo' dun heah Uncle Harvey tell yo' dat fo' dis ? "

" Yes, I have heard you say that, Uncle Harvey, many a time, but what sort of a thing is a hant, anyhow ? "

" Well, honey, sum say dey looks lek one thing, and sum say dey looks lek nuther, but de one I seed long yer one night, wuz lek a hoss, ceptin' hit never had no hed on, and de man wha was on 'im neber had no hed on 'im nuther; but de man had a sode in e belt, and spurs on e heel, an' 'stid er ridin' lek yuther folks, he rid wid his face tods de hosses tail."

The little boy said, " Uncle Harvey, I thought you said the man did not have any head. How could you see which way his face was ? "

" Well, I do declar' to goodness, ef yo' aint de out doinest chil' in dis worl'. Aint I dun tol' yo' dat hant had on spurs, an sode in e belt, an' of cose, yo' know which way he face wuz, ef e had any face; an' de hoss dun mek no noise wid e feet when he walk; en wen yo' stop, e stop, an wen yo' start, e start; an' e don' get no closer, ner no furder, en e jes foller yo' eber whar yo' go; an' yo' can't tech 'im, en yo' can't heah 'im; but eber whar yo' go, dar he is."

Just at this juncture Uncle Harvey's story was cut short by some one hid in a ditch close by the roadside, saying, " Halt."

" Who dat say halt," replied Uncle Harvey. Just

then two shots rang out, bang! bang! Uncle Harvey struck out in a trot and said, " I's er gwine ter have yo' up fur dat." Bang! bang! went two more shots and the burning tow-wads from the gun fell close to Uncle Harvey's feet. By this time he was in a full run, having already caught the Little Boy by the hand. He never waited for any further invitations to halt, nor for any further conversation, but we went as fast as our feet would carry us. Uncle Harvey, being very fat, was soon out of breath and was puffing like a wind-broken horse. The Little Boy was not scared of course, for he knew it was " Willum and Sildum," having already previously arranged with them that he would tell Uncle Harvey they had gone to Smyth's School-house.

The Little Boy said, " Uncle Harvey, that must have been ' bushwhackers.' "

" Dem's no bushwhackers, honey, dem's Klu Kluxes; dat's wat hit is—haint I dun seed 'em wid my own eyes—cum on yer, honey, taint no time ter talk; dey will git us fo' we gits to de school-house sho'."

So we went on as fast as we could to the school-house. When we got there, Uncle Harvey was so near out of wind, that he couldn't speak, but just sat behind the door and puffed like a steam-engine, and the perspiration was streaming down his black shiny face.

The preacher was just in the midst of a very fervent prayer. So, owing to the preacher's prayer and the other brethren shouting "Amen," supplemented by Uncle Harvey's puffing—which all in the house ascribed to religious emotion, the little school-house was in quite a commotion. As soon as the prayer was over, Uncle Harvey managed to get one of the men outside, and tell him of the occurrence. I have always regretted I did not hear this conversation, but suffice it to say, the brother came in and announced that bushwhackers were in the neighborhood, and that it would be wise to dismiss the congregation. Uncle Harvey and the Little Boy were the heroes of the evening, having just escaped death from the bushwhackers, and Uncle Harvey showed them sundry holes in his clothing which he vowed had been made by "bulits."

Curiously enough, in his excitement he never missed "Willum and Sildum" from church, and he told them when we got home about his narrow escape.

"Now chillens, dese yer is sutenly skeery times, and Unk Harvey out er huntin' yo' and yer yo' is er settin' in de house all de time. I declar' fo' de Lawd, yo' is de beatinest chillens eber I seed. I don' know wat er gwine ter cum er yo' atter Unk Harvey dun dead an' gone. De Klu Klux, er bushwhackers, er de hants, er sumpin' will sholy git yo'. Now yo'

71

is dum-pintedly heah'd wat Unk Harvey is got ter say."

The joke by this time had assumed such a serious aspect in the community that it was several weeks before we told how we had broken up the meeting.

Uncle Harvey has been dead many years, but his quaint stories and Christian character are fresh in the memory of many men and women, who, as children, loved to hear him talk and sing and pray.

THE CABIN IN THE WOODS

THERE is a plant that grows in Mexico which has a strange effect upon people. When any one comes into the vicinity where it grows, he immediately loses his " bearings." He does not know where he is, nor which way to go, but feels a sense of bewilderment until he gets away from its influence. I do not know of any herb of this kind in Southwest Virginia, but I do know, or used to know, of a weird spot in the mountains that had a similar effect upon one. This place was on the top of one of the foothills of Walker's Mountain, in the midst of the thickest, heaviest forest of white oaks and poplars, and far away from any house or public road.

There was, on top of this knoll, a sort of tableland of about half an acre, covered with a compact sod of native blue-grass. There had once been a cabin there, judging from what seemed to be the ruins of an old building of some kind, and there were a few old peach trees, and the trunk of an old apple tree still standing. The knoll was flat on top and sloped away symmetrically on all sides. The grass grew even and smooth, and always looked as if it had been mown with a lawn-mower. At the foot of the hill, on one side, ran a small creek; on another side was a " freestone " spring, the only one known to be in existence in this limestone country; on another side was an opening to a cave; and on the side opposite to the mouth of the cave, was a " scoop out " in the ground, covered with a smooth, beautiful growth of blue-grass. Not a weed or flower, or a sprig grew here, though wild flowers were abundant everywhere else on the mountain sides; but no matter how long-continued was a drouth in summer, this place looked as if favored by constant showers. Why the grass never grew tall and why no other growth dared show itself, I cannot say. It was the most silent spot in the world. I never saw a bird or squirrel, or even an insect, on this spot of ground, and, indeed, one rarely ever heard or saw anything of the kind in the woods nearby, though I have occasionally seen a pheasant along the creek. I visited this spot a number of times when I was a boy. You could lie on this turf and be absolutely sure of not being disturbed by insects, or bugs, while you watched the blue sky, or the fleecy white clouds that floated above you. It was a place of absolute quiet and solitude.

But the strangest thing about this place was that you could go there and sit or lie down for awhile, and when you got up to leave, you could not tell for the life of you which way you came in, although you had the spring, and the cave, and the creek for landmarks. In spite of yourself, the question would always arise, which is the right way out? This would happen not only occasionally, but always, and not only with one person, but with every one. I have reasoned and puzzled over this, but never reached a solution of it.

But there was a still stranger thing about this place. I had two faithful dogs, almost human in intelligence, and as obedient to me as dogs could be. They would follow me into this place, but I could not keep them there. They would lie down for a few moments, but soon becoming restless would go off, and lie in the woods nearby. When I called them back, they would come, but I could not keep them long before they again showed signs of restlessness, and would get up and leave me. Into that cave they would not go, though they would go into any other hole willingly at my bidding. In fact I have never known of any animal running into the cave, though I have known of them coming out. Even foxes chased by the hounds sought no refuge there. I have seen the fox-hounds run foxes all over the surrounding woods, but never knew a fox or rabbit to run into that hole. I never knew the cause of this; there was no peculiar odor about the place, nor any peculiar sensation felt, except that of loneliness and solitude.

It was on this spot, years afterward, that " Old Witch Mary " lived. She was as strange and weird a character as the spot on which she dwelt. How she got her cabin built on this spot no one was ever able to tell definitely, though there were many theories about it; but, anyway, her cabin was there and may be there to this day, although poor old Witch Mary has long since passed away. Her end was as mysterious and uncanny as her hut that stood on this enchanted spot.

It was supposed that the negroes in the country had built the cabin for her in a single night; that they had the timber cut, and by a preconcerted plan had met on some particular night and put together this building for Mary. But why they did so, no one could even suggest a reason; and why they built it on the enchanted or " Haunted Knoll," as they called it, was still more remarkable; for they were not only afraid of Witch Mary, but they were exceedingly superstitious about this spot. Then, why or how they could have been induced to go there in the night and build this hut, was something hard to explain. No one of the negroes was ever known to do otherwise than to deny that they ever had anything to do with it.

Another theory was that some white men built

"This mysterious hut stood there for years."

this hut for Mary, and had done it for the purpose of keeping the negroes in awe of her, for they believed she could " Hoodoo " them, and could tell any secret in the world, if she desired to do so. If anything was stolen or lost in the community, or any mysterious thing happened, Mary could tell all about it, provided she desired to do so. It was, therefore, supposed by some that white people had built this cabin for Witch Mary. But, conjectures aside, one thing was certain; Mary had the cabin, and no one ever knew by whom or when it was built. The white people said the negroes built it, the negroes said the Indians had come back and built it and stole away in the night. Old Mary said, " De angels flew down from de skies while I was asleep on de ground, an' wen I wake up de cabin wuz standin' over me." This was all she would ever tell.

So this mysterious hut, built on this enchanted spot, for this weird, eccentric, and queer little, old black woman stood there for years as Mary's home, and for years after her death also it was believed to be " a haunted house," and there were many queer stories in vogue about it. Many a time have the children, white and black, been made to tremble with fear by the tales told by the black Mammies about Witch Mary and this hut. All that was necessary to make children take castor-oil, or any other bad medicine, was to tell them that old Witch Mary was coming to get them and take them away to her cabin in the woods. The oil would be immediately swallowed and no crying or fussing heard. If a negro was sick in the negro quarters, " Witch Mary " was supposed to have something to do with it, and yet, she was loved and respected by all the white people, and loved and feared by all the negroes.

If any of the little pickaninnies were sick, " Mary " could cure them with her herbs and her incantations. If they died. Mary was the cause of their death.

Mary was also sometimes called " Free Mary," because she did not belong to any one. Witch Mary's, or Free Mary's, cabin was always nice and clean, and everything in perfect order. She had thousands of bunches of herbs and little bags of leaves hung up all around the walls, and she made her decoctions of herbs for all the different diseases that the negroes had. Some of her medicine must have been efficacious, for she could beyond a doubt cure any sort of snake bites. She was sent for far and near, if any one was snake-bitten, and she always effected a cure; at least, no one ever died from snake bite after Mary had administered some of her snake medicine, and had applied some of the leaves to the bite.

Once there were some horses stolen from a farmer in the community which could nowhere be traced. On conferring with Mary, she told the farmer that his horses had been ridden in the night to a certain place in an adjoining county and turned loose; that the thieves had gone on; that the horses would all be found there, except one; that that one would never be found, and that the man who stole it was not in possession of it. The horses were found as she predicted.

She always said that at the foot of the mountain, a half a mile from her cabin, there was silver and lead in abundance, but she would never say where the spot was. She further maintained that it was not best for the men of this generation to know it; that it was put there for people of another generation; and that for this reason she would not tell where it was. This statement was made a short time before her death.

Many such things she told, and very often she was correct in her predictions. How she foretold future events, and how she could tell past events unknown to others was as strange as her life.

Uncle Andy and the Little Boy went one day to her cabin to ask her where some hogs could be found, which had disappeared from the farm (no negro was ever known to go to Mary's cabin alone). She very promptly said in answer to our inquiry:

"Wat yo' cum yere fo', axin' 'bout de hogs, wen de hogs is at de barn asleep in de straw."

Uncle Andy said, "Mary, yo' knows dem hogs is

not dar; dey bin gone fer fo' weeks; dey is not gwine
ter lay in de straw fo' weeks, dat yo' knows."

" Dey not bin layin' dar fur fo' weeks; dey has bin
dar des a little while." This is all she would say
about the hogs. Thereupon she took the Little Boy
on her lap, looked into his face for a long time, then
put her hands on his head, and said:

" Mary's time yer is mighty nigh up—dis is de
las' time she'l see dis pretty black head, en' dese
pretty black eyes. Mary wuz in de skies, en' she
seed de place whar she is gwine—dar wuz some beautiful chillen dar, en' dey wuz all ez happy ez de day
wuz long. Mary will spend her time dar playin'
wid dem little chillen, en' bathin' dem in de crystal
water—de water dar is so bright an' clear, an' de
flowers is so sweet! Mary seed de very chillens whar
is to cum fur her—some is black en' some is white;
dey is gwine ter bring de flowers to put on Mary's
po' ole wrinkled body, en' den Mary will be gone
from dis house, en' Mary won't tell nobody fo' she
go whar de silver is. It is deep in de groun', en' de
cave en' de spring has secrets, but Mary aint gwine
tell yo' now. Dis is de las' time I's gwine to see yo'
face, honey. I is tole Andy whar is de hogs—dis is
de las' secret Mary is gwine ter tell on dis yearth."

" Come on, honey," said Andy. " Les go long
outen dis yer place—tain no time to be foolin' wid
Mary. She don't know no mo' whar dem hogs is den

yo' does; en' sides dat, Mary dun gone ter talkin' 'bout de yuther worl', an' Andy do'n lack dat kine er talk no how. I is gwine outen dis place."

"Well, good-bye, Andy," said Mary, "an' good-bye ter yo', honey." Mary will be waitin' fo' yo' when yo' comes ter see her."

With this she sat down on the ground, and we could not get her to say another word, nor even look at us; her thoughts seemed to be somewhere else.

We hurried out of the woods and journeyed homeward. Andy saying nothing until we were near our journey's end. Then he said, "Ole Witch Mary talk powful cu'uous dis ebenin.' I woner wat she studyn' 'bout now—she dun missed hit 'bout dem hogs do, dats sho'. How in de name of de Lawd she think dem hogs er gwine ter git in de barn lot in de straw en' nobody see em—dat ole woman dun los' her mine at las',—Andy dun said she wuz crazy, now he know it. I is feared uv dat ole woman anyhow, en' I aint gwine back dar no mo', hogs er no hogs."

As we were about reaching home, we met one of the little negroes who called, "Unc Andy, de hogs dun come home, an' is en de barn yard er layin' in de straw pile." Uncle Andy said, "Don't dat beat de debil; dats jes wat ole Mary said—how in de name of de Lawd do she know dem hogs wuz dar; dat beats me sho'. I aint gwine 'bout dat ole woman narry nuther time."

Three days after this poor old Witch Mary was found dead in her cabin, her body covered with withered flowers. Who had been there and brought the flowers was never known, but true to her prophecy, the old woman had gone from earth to bathe in the crystal water. Mary's hut, this strange spot of ground, the old woman herself, and her strange life and death, were always a mystery to those who knew her, and remain so to this day.

THE BLIND FIDDLER

IN the thickening shadows of the evening a young man walked leisurely down the path that led to the front porch of an old-fashioned farm-house. The honeysuckle almost obscured the front of the house as they hung thick on the lattice work that ran almost entirely around it. They were in full bloom, and the fragrance so strong that the gentle summer wind carried it on its breath for more than a mile. The moon was full and had just peeped over the hilltop in front of the house, and looked like a crown of silver on the head of some great giant.

The young man walked up to the front door and rapped as he had done many times before, and waited patiently for a response from the Blind Fiddler to " Come in."

Failing to receive the usual response to his knock, he repeated it, and stood waiting in the silence, until the hum from the wings of the moths and myriads of insects in the honeysuckle sounded like distant music. The weird notes of a screech owl from the old oak tree that stood in the front yard gave the young man a decidedly lonely feeling, though these were familiar sounds from his earliest recollection.

Still not receiving any response to his knock, he ventured to try the door. It yielded and he threw it open wide, and the full-orbed moon shone squarely in the door from over the hilltop, and filled the room with a soft, uncertain light, rendering the objects in the room visible, but indistinct. The only sound was the lonely chirp of a cricket from somewhere near the old stone hearth.

He stood irresolute for a moment, uncertain whether to enter or not, but finally did so.

"Uncle Dan!" he called. No response save the chirp of the cricket on the hearth. As his eyes became more accustomed to the darkness of the room he could see the chairs, but none were occupied. The bed stood in the corner in a deeper shadow; he could see the white counterpane and some dark object on the bed.

Being filled with superstitious dread, he almost screamed, "Uncle Dan!"

"What's the matter, my boy? Is the house on fire?" came the response.

"Why no, but you frightened me out of my wits; it was so quiet in here, and so lonely, and no sound but the hum of the insects in the honeysuckle and the chirp of the cricket on the hearth, and so dark I could not see you. I was afraid you might be dead."

"No light in the room, dark, and dead," the Blind

Fiddler repeated after him. "Did it ever occur to you," said he, "that there is never any light in the room for me? No matter how bright the sun shines, nor how the silver moonbeams light up the room, it is always dark to me. I do not know why I have the lamp lighted at night; it gives no light to me. The world is as dark to me, my boy, at noon as it is at midnight. The golden sunshine and the silver moonlight are all the same to me—one eternal night."

"Oh, Uncle Dan! don't talk that way. Let me light the lamp. I can't stay in this dark room. I am sure it will seem brighter to you anyway."

The young man lit the lamp, and with the light his heart also grew lighter.

"Uncle Dan," he said, "play some on the violin for me. I came over to hear you play. It will be the last time I will hear you before I go to college again. I am sure I would be willing to be blind to be able to play the violin like you can."

"Nothing can take the place of sight, my boy. Those who can see cannot realize, or begin to think what it means to be blind. No man can tell you what it means. Darkness—everlasting darkness—is all you can see. Did you ever wake up in the night in a dark room, open your eyes, and try to look about you, try to see, and the only thing you can see is blackness? You turn your head every way, and strain your eyes to see, but every way you look all is blackness. You hear the voices of your friends and loved ones speaking out of blackness. You hear the birds singing and the wind blowing; you hear the water ripple and smell perfume of the flowers; you hear the lowing of the herd, the bleating of the lambs, and the busy sounds from fowls in the barnyard. You hear the droning of the drowsy beetle, the chirp of the cricket and the grasshopper, the hum of the bees, and the busy insect world. You hear the crash of the thunder and the roar of the winds. You hear the summer breeze as it whispers through the leaves and kisses the petals of the blushing flowers and steals away laden with their perfume. You hear all the sounds from the busy marts of trade, and all the sweet sounds from the voices of nature from whatever source they come, but they all come from the bosom of utter darkness, from the world of eternal night. Can you understand what I mean, my boy?"

The blind man sat musing for a time, then took up the violin and rapped on it with the bow, as was his custom, and began to play a piece of his own composition, which he called the "Prayer Meeting," in imitation of the exhortation, the song, and the prayer.

It was a remarkable production. How he could imitate with the strings the voices, the songs and the prayers to such perfection was marvellous.

After playing this piece, he laid down the violin and fell into a reverie.

" Uncle Dan, are you asleep ? "

" No, my boy; only walking in the spirit. I do not want you to feel gloomy from what I said to you about being blind. I can see with my spiritual eyes. I see the new heaven and the new earth. It won't be long until God will wipe away all tears from my face, and these scales will fall from my eyes, and I will see the Holy City, the New Jerusalem, prepared as a bride for her husband; all things shall be made new. I will see the great City, having the glory of God, and it's light will be like a jasper stone, clear as crystal; the foundations thereof will be garnished with all precious stones; the gates will be pearl, and the streets pure gold. There will be no need of a sun, neither the moon shall shine: the glory of God will light it. I am blind, my boy, but I can see. God's grace and love is sufficient for me. I am contented with my lot. I would not exchange places with the richest man in the world and have my sight restored, if it would rob me of this ' peace that passeth all understanding.' "

Within a few days the young man had gone to a medical college to complete his course. He had been very skeptical in his views, and was inclined, as are many young medical men, to be atheistic. His last visit to the Blind Fiddler's house, and his conversation with him, had made a deep impression on him. He had many times gone over in his mind the beautiful faith and trust this blind man had in God, and how it alone sustained him and made him content and happy, even in his terrible affliction.

It was a raw and gusty night in March, nearing the close of the session. The young student, in his black gown, was seated on a stool in the dissecting room on the fifth floor of the building. It was two o'clock in the night, and all the other students had long since gone down, but he had determined to remain and finish the dissection he was doing, if it took him until daylight. Even the restless crowds on the busy streets far below had grown quiet. He was making a delicate dissection and absorbed in his work.

There were seven subjects (stiffs) on the tables. The one at the farther side of the room and nearest the window had been brought in that night, and had a towel thrown over the face, which had not been removed.

While he was busy with his work he heard a slight noise at the farther side of the room. He glanced around, but saw nothing, and concluded it was a rat, as they sometimes infest dissecting rooms. In a short while he again heard the same noise; but still seeing nothing, continued his work. He was not afraid, but overwork and loss of sleep had made him slightly nervous. Hearing the noise the third time, he got down from his stool and went the rounds, looking at each dead body as he passed the tables on

which they lay. Each face was as familiar to him as
the faces of the boys that were dissecting them.
There they lay as silent as the tomb. Finding nothing, he had returned to his work, when suddenly there
was a rattle and a crash that made him jump from
his seat and stand staring across the room, but everything was quiet.

Again he went to the farther side of the room to see
what had made the crash, and to his relief he discovered that the janitor had set a pan of bones which
he had been cleaning on the end of the curtain in
the window, which was down from the top, and when
a gust of wind came it lifted the side of the pan,
which dropped back with a rattle until finally a
stronger breeze came, upsetting the pan with a rattle
and bang on the floor.

He picked up the bones, replaced them in the pan,
set them back in the window, and turned around to
the table that stood behind him, lifting the towel from
the face of the cadaver. Imagine, if you can, his
surprise to see the face of the Blind Fiddler, his
friend, before him. He could not believe his own
eyes; he turned on all the electric lights; there could
be no mistake. There were the sightless orbs, and
every feature perfect, with a calm and peaceful look
on his face; even a smile seemed to be on his lips.
He was so shocked he could not yet believe it was his
friend; but he knew of a scar that he had in the palm

of his hand that would identify him beyond the shadow of a doubt. He examined the hand; the scar was there; there could be no mistake, it was his friend.

He hastily left the dissecting room and went to his own room, where he had not been since morning, and threw himself in a chair to collect his thoughts. His last visit and the conversation of the Blind Fiddler were as plain to him as if they had just happened. There was an inexpressible satisfaction to him to remember the beautiful faith he had in God. Now those blind eyes could see, and those dead lips spoke to him from the darkness, from the blackness.

He arose from his seat and discovered some letters that had been put on his table during his absence. One from home told of the sudden death and burial of the Blind Fiddler. All doubt was set at rest; but how could he have gotten there?

He announced to the college authorities the facts, and telegraphed home that the remains would be immediately returned. An examination of the graves of the quiet country cemetery revealed the fact that numbers of them were empty, which led to the unearthing of a gang of ghouls that had been robbing the graves.

When the remains returned a large crowd had assembled to attend the burial. The golden light of a brilliant sunset fell full into the grave, giving the already yellow earth an unusual brightness.

A solemn hush pervaded the throng, when suddenly there seemed to be sounds of faraway music, when all with one accord looked toward the sky, each face having depicted on it anticipation and surprise.

It was one of the most remarkable scenes ever witnessed, the silence and solemnity were oppressive, and to this day no one that was present ever refers to it except with awe and bated breath.

The Blind Fiddler was in the dissecting room, but spoke from Paradise. The medical student was skeptical, but the clouds have been brushed away.

AN ADVENTURE

THE Doctor's horse was lame; he had many calls to make and no horse. He was sitting on the front porch thinking what he would do, when Captain Chesterfield Smyth rode up to the gate. Everybody called him Captain. No one ever knew how he came by the title, unless it was because his father was a major, and he was, therefore, a captain by birth.

" Hello, Doctor! Don't you want to buy a horse? "

If there was anything the Doctor did want then it was a horse, but he did not think it the best policy to let the Captain know it.

" Well, hardly to-day, Captain. Get down and come in."

" No; you come out and look at this horse anyway. He is a fine saddler," said the Captain.

The Doctor walked leisurely down, leaned over the gate, and after awhile remarked:

" That is the first horse I ever saw that had a hind leg curved like half of a barrel hoop."

" All good saddle horses have crooked hind legs," said the Captain. " I never knew a horse with a leg like this that was not a good mover."

"Yes, but he is hogbacked. I don't want a horse with a back like that."

"Did you ever see a horse with a back like that, Doctor, that was not a good saddler? It's a sign I never knew to fail."

"Yes; but see how narrow he is in the chest and sharp between the fore legs. He's got no wind."

"A horse that is narrow between the fore legs never stumbles; they are all sure-footed; just the kind of a horse for a doctor."

"I had just as soon own a dromedary," said the Doctor.

"What in the devil is a dromedary? Are they imported horses? You can't find one that will beat this horse moving. Get on and try him."

The Doctor mounted and gave him a turn up and down the road, and was surprised to find that he did go surprisingly well.

"What's your price for him?" said the Doctor.

"My asking price is ninety dollars. I would take eighty," replied the Captain.

"Fifty dollars is a big price for him. I would give you thirty-five dollars," replied the Doctor, "and be sorry for that."

"Is that the best you could do for a horse like this? You don't want me to give you a horse, do you?"

The Doctor saw the Captain was going to take him up on the thirty-five dollar offer, and quickly added:

" I would not have him if you would give him to me."

The Captain had lost by not accepting the thirty-five dollar offer at once. He waited a moment, and seeing a cow in a lot nearby, said:

" How will you trade that cow for this horse? "

The Doctor had just taken the cow on a twelve-dollar debt. He replied:

" I will give you the cow for the horse."

" Give me five dollars to boot, and it's a trade."

" No," said the Doctor; " I will split the difference and give you two and a half."

" Well, being's it's you, Doc, I'll let him go at that; but you have burnt me up on this trade."

As the Captain started he turned, came back, and said:

" Doctor, there is one thing about that horse I forgot to tell you: his head swims when he crosses water, and he's apt to go down the river or lie down in the water with you. You will have to watch him on that point."

A good deal of the Doctor's practice being on the other side of the river, he was now convinced that the Captain had gotten the best of him.

That night, about twelve o'clock, someone called the Doctor. It was Arnett, who lived eight miles on the other side of the river. The Doctor saddled his new horse, and they set out. As they rode along the muddy roads at a slow pace, Arnett was singing and talking, the Doctor moody and silent.

They arrived at last, cold and muddy. The lamp was still burning, but the fire had died down to a few smouldering embers. Arnett soon had a bright blaze going, and when the Doctor had warmed a little, he said:

"Bill, where is the patient?"

"I gad, it's me," he replied.

The Doctor was not sure he understood him. He repeated the question.

"It's me, I say."

"Well, I don't understand you. You don't mean to say it is you that is burnt?"

"Yes, I do; it's *me*."

"Are you crazy? You don't mean you came after me and had me ride eight miles over these roads with you to see you?"

"Yes, I do. I am the one that's burnt."

"Well, let's see the burn."

Bill proceeded to pull up the right leg of his trousers, and sure enough, the entire calf of his leg was cooked. It was so hard when the Doctor tapped it with an instrument it sounded like rapping on a dry board.

"Well, how did you do that, and why did you come after me and have me ride eight miles to see you when you were already at my office?"

" Well, I'll tell you the truth, Doc. I was drunk and laid down before the fire, and a chunk fell down against my leg while I was asleep, and when I woke up I was singing, ' Fire in the mountains, run, boys, run.' I put the fire out and started for the Doctor to come to see me; and here you are, and I want you to do something for me. It hurts like the devil."

The Doctor was too mad to appreciate the joke. He dressed the burn without comment, and hastily left the house and started back home, " mad as a March hare."

He had forgotten all about his new horse when he came to the ford of the river. The river was shallow at the ford, and not far from bank to bank. He rode in, absorbed in thinking of the absurd thing he had just done, and was only called to his senses by the unusual length of time it was taking him to reach the opposite bank, when it occurred to him what Captain Smyth had told him about the horse's head swimming when he crossed water.

He realized that he must have gotten below the ford and was going down the river. He stopped and tried to peer into the darkness to see the other bank, but could see nothing.

About this time the horse developed the other trait he had been warned of by the Captain, and started to lie down. The Doctor became excited; he drove the spurs into the horse's side, turned his head to-

wards the bank, and felt relieved when he found he
had reached dry land.

He got down and led the horse to see if he could
find the road, and was surprised to find that he came
to the water's edge again. He turned around, went
the other direction, and very soon the same condition
confronted him; every way he went he came to water.
He was bewildered, and sat down to think, arriving
at the conclusion that the horse had gone down the
river, and that he was now on a small island. He
located the north star, and wisely concluded his course
was south, having entered the ford on the north bank.

He was revolving in his mind the advisability of
waiting for day, although he was wet and cold, when
he heard the growl of distant thunder. Looking to
the west, he saw dark clouds gathering; there was
going to be a storm. He knew it would not do to wait
any longer, as the mountain streams rose very rapidly
during a heavy storm.

Leading his horse to the bank, he mounted, fixed
himself well in the saddle, and put spurs to him. He
hesitated, drew back, wheeled about, reared and refused to go in; but by whip and spur he finally made
the plunge and went in up to the saddle.

The Doctor was alarmed; he had not expected this;
but there was nothing to do but trust to luck and push
ahead, when, to his great relief, he found the water
getting shallow, and in a few moments he struck the

bank. He could have shouted. Columbus was no happier when he set foot on American soil than was the Doctor when his " light-headed " horse set hoof on that solid ground.

Though the storm was rapidly approaching, and he was cold and wet to the skin, and his saddle pockets with the medicine gone to physic the fishes, he did not care. He soon found the road that led from the river through a long, dark gorge called " Dead Man's Hollow." It was said that a man had been murdered in this gulch many years ago and the place was haunted; but the Doctor felt so much relieved at his escape from the river that he thought nothing of the dark, gloomy gulch and grewsome stories he had heard of " Dead Man's Hollow."

He thought it must be true that the " darkest hours are just before dawn," for the darkness was intense; the clouds had thickened, the thunder had grown more distinct, the storm would soon be on.

He urged his horse along as fast as he could with safety, when he begun to hear the leaves rustle and the twigs crack, as if some animal was walking in the leaves near him. He peered into the darkness, but saw nothing, but keeping his eyes turned in the direction of the sound, he presently saw what appeared to be two balls of fire, evidently the eyes of some wild animal, following him. He shouted at the top of his voice, hoping to frighten it away; but the blazing eyes only seemed to stand still.

He urged his horse, which now appeared to be thoroughly frightened, when suddenly he stopped, and he could feel him quivering in every muscle. Urge as he would with whip and spur he would not budge. The air seemed to have a strange chill about it, and he heard the animal, whatever it was, bound away through the brush.

He put his hand down on his horse's shoulder; he was trembling like a leaf and wet with sweat. There seemed to be something awful about to happen. Glancing over his shoulder, he either saw, or thought he saw, a long, bony hand on each of his shoulders; and looking over his shoulder a face covered with long, white beard and head with snow-white hair, and in the sunken caverns of his face glowed two fiery eye-balls, like those he had seen on the mountain side.

He tried to scream; his voice had left him. He tried to spring from his trembling horse; he was as one paralyzed.

Suddenly there came a flash of lightning and a crash of thunder which shook the mountains to their very foundation; the horse sprang forward with a sudden bound, which came near throwing the Doctor to the ground.

By the flash of lightning he saw a white cow in the

road, which had evidently frightened the horse and made him stop.

The nearest house the other side of " Dead Man's Hollow " was Captain Smyth's. Day was just beginning to dawn when the Doctor rode up to the Captain's gate, got off, and knocked at the door. The genial Captain was up and had a big log fire burning in the old-fashioned fireplace.

He went to the door, and was surprised to find the Doctor his early visitor.

" Why, come in, Doctor. Where have you been this early in the morning, and what on earth is the white stuff you have all over your coat and your hat? You haven't been to mill this time of day, have you? And you are as pale as a ghost; are you sick? "

The Doctor was quick-witted. He saw at a glance what his ghost had been. He had laid his hat down in some flour which Arnett had been using on his burnt leg, and had gotten it on his coat and shoulders.

The blazing eyes of the catamount or wild cat he had just seen were photographed on the retina, and in the state of his excited nerves easily transferred to the face of the ghost of " Dead Man's Hollow," whose snowy beard and hair was his white hat brim, and his bony hands his flour-sprinkled shoulders. He said:

" Captain Smyth, I am cold. You usually keep a little apple brandy. Can you give me a toddy? "

101

"Why, certainly, Doctor. I have just had one myself, and will join you in another."

After the Doctor had gotten his toddy and had warmed by the log fire he told the Captain about the trick Arnett had played him, avoiding any reference to the river or "Dead Man's Hollow" incident.

The Captain said:

"Doctor, are you riding the horse you got from me? How do you like him? I hope you found no trouble with him at the river."

The Doctor replied:

"Oh, we got along very well considering how dark it was. He took me over and brought me back safe and sound. He travels well. How do you like the cow?"

"Doc, she can outkick a mule. My wife told me to take her back to you—that a 'light-headed horse' was better than a 'kicking cow.' I reckon you wouldn't trade back, would you?"

"Not without boot, Captain. The horse is all you represented him to be, and more. I will trade back with you for twenty-five dollars to boot."

The trade was closed; the Doctor got the cow and twenty-five dollars to buy some new saddle bags. The Captain got his horse back to swap with someone else.

In the years that have passed they have spent many a congenial hour over a bowl of hot apple toddy, discussing who got the best of the trade.

WHIPPED INTO MANHOOD

I.

AS I sit on my front porch and look out on the grand old Iron Mountain, as it lifts itself above the vapor that hangs lazily upon its sides, I am carried back twenty years to a lonely cove, where the rays of the sun are shut out by the dense foliage, and where a bright and bubbling spring of pure cold water leaps from its rocky bed and dashes off in its wild chase down the mountain side, through the pine-clad ridges to the broad valley below, spreading out like an ocean of green.

In this lonely cove resided for many years Wilson Guy, a benefactor of his race. He was one-fourth Indian, as straight as the pines under which he lived, active and athletic, an everlasting friend to those he loved, an unrelenting foe to those he hated. He was a man of strong passions, reckless and fond of adventures.

Being a man of unusual strength, and absolutely fearless, he was dangerous when excited or laboring under a sense of real or supposed injury.

His father was a French Huguenot, of whom very

little was known, having deserted his wife and left for parts unknown.

"His mother was a half-breed Catawba Indian, with all the characteristics of a full Indian. She had long, glossy, black hair, that reached nearly to the floor when she stood erect; was a remarkably handsome woman with a superb figure. She was amiable, loving and affectionate, except when aroused or angered; then she was a perfect demon, as fierce as a wounded tigress. It was supposed her husband deserted her on this account."

It was from this parentage that Wilson Guy sprang, and it is little to be wondered at that he inherited strange characteristics.

He was the only person I ever knew who possessed the remarkable combination of human intelligence and animal instinct. Being endowed with this peculiar power it was almost impossible to deceive him. He detested what he considered a cowardly act, or taking an unfair advantage of an enemy, even if an animal.

To illustrate: On one occasion he found the trail of a large bear, and true to his instinct, he followed it patiently and persistently up mountain sides and through mountain gorges, and along dangerous mountain passes, where it would seem nothing but a wild animal could go, till, turning a large boulder that jutted out from the mountain side, he came suddenly upon his game, a large black bear, lying on a ledge of rock fast asleep.

There is no other animal that sleeps as soundly as a bear. It is sometimes difficult to awaken them. There he lay curled up in a ball, looking like a huge bundle of black fur.

Instead of using his gun and dispatching him as he lay quietly sleeping he, without hesitation, drew from his belt his tomahawk and struck him a heavy blow on one of his huge paws as it lay upon the rock, disdaining the cowardly act, as he conceived it, of killing his game while sleeping.

" Instantly his powerful adversary sprang up, and he found himself face to face in a hand-to-hand combat with the bear. In too close quarters to use his gun, he threw it to the ground and used his tomahawk.

" For a few moments they took it lick about like two pugilists, he making every lick count and dodging skillfully each blow of the bear. While the combat was going on the bear was all the while slowly retreating towards a precipice some distance away, from the brink of which he could leap into the tree-tops below and make his escape, and finally made a rush for it, when the hunter seized him by the hair and mounted him.

" Having dropped his tomahawk, his only weapon left was his hunting knife. Holding on with his left hand he drew his knife from his belt and plunged it into the bear's side, just behind the fore-shoulder, when he dropped like he had been shot, just as he reached the edge of the precipice. His head and fore-paws were hanging over—one foot farther and they would have gone hundreds of feet down the jagged rocks, when the career of Wilson Guy would have come to a close."

But such was not to be the end of this brave, reckless, cunning, dangerous and, strange to say, this intensely *pious* man.

His father having deserted his mother when he was a babe, and his mother having died when he was a mere boy, he had been raised by a family of white people, who taught him in their simple way the story of the Nazarene.

Being a child of nature, true to his Indian instincts, he heard the voice of God in the whispering of the summer winds, and in the roar of the winter storms. He heard Him in the songs of the birds, and saw Him in the lightning's glare. He worshipped Him in the red glow of the evening sunset, and in the pink hue of the morning's dawn. He heard Him in the rush of the mountain torrent, and saw Him in the flash of its crystal water. He worshipped Him in his lonely cabin, and knelt reverently on the mountain cliffs. No time or place was the wrong time or the wrong place for him to worship God.

" The earth is the Lord's and the fullness thereof,

and all that dwell therein," was his creed. But his motto was in accord with his Indian nature: Do unto others as they do unto you—" An eye for an eye, and a tooth for a tooth."

II.

James Thompson, the humble woodsman with whom he went to live after the death of his mother, had an only daughter, Martha, several years his junior. They grew up together as brother and sister. He was wont to pluck for her the first ripe grapes from the rugged cliffs and the first blossoms of the wild honeysuckle and geraniums. He would carry her on his shoulder over the rough and dangerous mountain paths, and tell her in the winter evenings by the light wood fire the stories of his boyish imagination of bears and wolves, till her cheeks would burn and she would look with frightened eyes at the door, and beg him not to tell her any more such " scarey tales," then would slip off to bed and cover up her golden head, to shut out the frightful scenes.

Thus it was they lived together and spent their childhood days, and he saw her bloom like a wild rose from childhood into womanhood, and she in turn learned to love and depend on him as her elder brother.

Martha Thompson was the most beautiful woman I have ever seen. Her eyes were as blue as the summer skies. Her hair was a color that cannot well be described. It was a dark, rich chestnut auburn, and the only hair I ever saw that sparkled in the sunshine. When standing erect and flowing loose it touched the floor, and was as wavy as curly walnut. Her skin was exceedingly fair, and was the color of a pink rose leaf, except when she blushed—then it had the red tinge of coral blown into the pink. Her teeth were perfect, and their pure whiteness made a beautiful contrast with her red and delicately curved lips. Her nose was of perfect Grecian mould, and her left cheek when she smiled had a deep dimple, which left the merest trace when her face was composed. Her chin was the only feature that was not faultless. Her figure was superb, and every motion one of grace. She was graceful from her very cradle. She could no more help being graceful than she could keep from breathing. Her character was as beautiful and lovely as her person.

Such was Martha Thompson when I first saw her, and when her foster brother left her home to shift for himself in the nearby mountain in hunting and trapping.

His visits back to his adopted home were frequent, and he kept Martha well supplied with furs. The floor of her room was carpeted with bear skins, and he told his " White Lily," as he now called her, of his *real* adventures.

III.

In a broad, spreading valley, where the Holston River wound like a silver thread through the green fields, and beneath the weeping willows there lived a prosperous farmer, whose red and white and spotted cattle made a beautiful and real picture as they grazed, dotting the green meadows here and there, and stood in the cool water up to their knees in the hot summer days, or browsed lazily under the shade of the trees.

He was very wealthy and had an only son, then twenty years of age, on whose education he had spent thousands of dollars. He had sent him to high schools, colleges and universities, and had succeeded at last in educating him in athletics and in the high art of spending money in the most approved style of a regular college sport. He was an expert football player, and knew how to wear his hair long and shaggy. He could twirl the ball and bat a curve. He could pull the oars with the best of them, and with the boxing gloves he was second to none. He was leader of the Glee Club, and at poker, billiard and pool he was at home. He was handsome and of fine physique—*an all-round college sport.*

During his vacations he had found the humble home of James Thompson and met his daughter Martha. Being attracted by her beauty, he at once made up his mind that this mountain nymph, as he called her, should contribute to his luxurious tastes and pleasures during his leisure months at home.

Martha being young and having never been thrown in the society of young men, was naturally very much pleased with the attentions of this handsome young college man, whose gentle manners were so pleasing. He made her handsome presents and sang his college songs, much to her pleasure and delight. She trusted him as she had done her foster brother, learning to look for his coming, and was unhappy and disappointed when the summers came if he did not soon come to see her. He would take long hunts with her foster brother, and made him presents of guns and pistols and hunting knives.

But the animal instincts of Wilson Guy made him suspicious when Julian was with the " White Lily." He was not jealous of her as a lover, but he feared for her happiness, for when Julian was away at school he could see the shadows on her face and her merry laugh was not the same. Her life was changed. He began to regret that the " White Lily " had ever seen Julian, though he never suspected him of any wrong. His Indian nature bound him fast and true to a friend from whom he had accepted gifts and hospitality.

The time had again arrived for Julian's home-coming, and he brought with him a college mate to spend the vacation. They very soon came on a visit to Martha's home, and brought a tent to spend a few days in camp life in the mountains. It was during this visit that Wilson's eyes were opened and he saw the false game his friend was playing with Martha. He heard him say one night as he lay in his tent talking to his companion:

" Of course I do not intend to marry the mountain nymph, but I will make her think it is marriage, and it will be all the same to me, as I expect to leave for Europe to attend a German university, and will be absent for three years, and by that time she would be reconciled."

Then and there Wilson made up his mind to save Martha. The Indian sought his revenge. On the following day, when they were alone in the mountain on a trout stream fishing, he told Julian what he had overheard. Julian replied:

" You dog, you were sneaking about my tent in the night eavesdropping, were you ? "

Wilson replied, " The dog watches the wolf in sheep's clothing. I have killed many a wolf in these mountains."

" Yes," retorted Julian, " I have thrashed many a dog, and I'll thrash another one now for prowling abut my tent at night and stealing my secrets."

He felt perfectly sure of whipping Wilson, being a trained athlete and boxer. He made a fierce blow for Wilson's face, but as quick as a cat he dodged the blow, and Julian only struck the air, and with such force that he staggered forward, when Wilson tripped him and he plunged head first into the stream below.

"Cold water is bad for a mad wolf. Come out and dry yourself in the sun," said Wilson.

"I'll warm myself with the pleasant exercise of thrashing you, you half-breed dog!" replied Julian.

With this he made a rush for Wilson, who again skillfully side-stepped and struck him a powerful blow between the shoulders, knocking him flat on his face, when he leaped upon him with both feet, completely knocking the breath out of him.

He ran quickly to a leatherwood tree that stood near, and with his hunting knife peeled the bark off, twisting it into a rope, and tied his hands behind him, and bound his feet together. Then he went to the creek and brought water and bathed his head and face till he was restored to consciousness. He then bound him to a tree and made a whip of the bark.

Julian said, "Why have you bound me with these thongs and tied me to this tree?"

"When I get this whip made," said Wilson, "I am going to thrash the 'mad wolf' within an inch of his life for his cruel and unfaithful treatment of the 'White Lily.'"

"If you strike me one blow with that whip," said Julian, "I will shoot you like the dog that you are!"

112

"You seem to bark very loud for a wolf that cannot bite. When you had your hands and feet free why didn't you use them to some purpose? You were as awkward as a bear. You could do nothing if you were free but snap and run. You are a coward and a thief. You would steal the 'White Lily's' happiness and beauty and, like a cowardly thief, steal away across the ocean and leave her to pine and die. I'll thrash you with the whip and then leave you to die."

"You half-breed hound! don't you know if you strike me with a whip I will kill you?"

"I will strike you and see. A man that is coward enough to wrong an innocent and trusting girl, and then flee across the ocean, is too much of a coward to shoot another, unless he could do it when he was asleep or shoot him in the back. I'll strike you with the whip and then cut the thongs that bind you, and see what the cowardly wolf will do."

With this he struck him across the face with the whip, which left a mark as though he had burnt him with a hot iron. Then with his hunting knife he cut the thongs and freed him.

Julian was no coward whatever else he may have been, and the accident of his having fallen in the creek, and the humiliation of having been knocked down and bound, which he also considered an accident, in addition to having been struck in the face

113

with a whip, made his blood boil, and his first impulse was to shoot his adversary in his tracks; but he restrained himself while the Indian stood stolid and motionless, waiting for him to act.

"Why don't you shoot me, as you said you would if I struck you with the whip? The marks on your pale face will show for many a day that I kept my word."

"That death would be too easy," said Julian. "I want to punish you before I kill you, and prove to you I am not the coward you think I am. I challenge you to fight me a hand-to-hand fight, and after I have whipped you we will step ten paces and I will finish the job by shooting you."

Julian felt that with his years of training in boxing lessons and being the athlete he was it would be an easy matter to outdo this untrained half-breed. Then he took little risk in the pistol duel, since he could shoot the spots out of a card at ten steps as accurately as if they had been cut out.

The Indian very readily accepted the challenge. Julian went to the creek and bathed his face, still smarting and burning from the lash of the whip. The Indian stood motionless, waiting for him to announce his readiness for the combat.

Returning at last, he told him to prepare to defend himself, and the battle was on. Instead of knocking Wilson down, as he supposed he would do at the first pass, he found it impossible to strike him, he was so agile and quick of motion. He would avoid a blow as if by magic, till Julian found himself gradually losing strength, while the Indian did not seem in the least wearied.

Finally the Indian, as quick as a flash, in an unguarded moment rushed at Julian, and stooping, caught him below the knees and threw him over his head into the creek. The bone in Julian's right arm snapped like a pine stick.

When Julian came out he found it was useless to continue the fight with a broken arm. He said:

"You have won this fight. My right arm is broken; we will continue the fight with pistols."

He did not tell how frightfully his arm was broken and mangled. They selected their pistols, stepped the distance, and were preparing to fire when Julian fell in a faint. The Indian stood waiting, thinking it was some trick to catch him, but held his fire. Seeing Julian did not move, he went to him and found him unconscious. He ran to the creek, brought water, and was bathing his head when Martha Thompson, who knew nothing of what had been going on, appeared on the scene. She had been hunting for them for hours, with an important message for Julian. Seeing him on the ground and Wilson by his side, she ran to them. When she saw Julian's pale face with the red scar across it she exclaimed:

115

"What has happened?"

The Indian replied, "He is hurt."

She looked quickly at the Indian, but seeing nothing in his stolid face, she ran to the creek for more water. While she was gone Julian opened his eyes, and seeing her coming with the water, said to the Indian:

"Promise me you will not tell her what has happened."

The Indian bowed his head in assent. Martha again said:

"What has happened? How did you get hurt?"

"I fell and have broken my arm."

They attempted to lift him into a sitting posture, and again he fainted. The blood was flowing freely. They hastily cut open the sleeve and found the bone driven through the flesh, and the blood spurting in jets. An artery had been wounded. The Indian bound it tightly with the leatherwood thong and stopped the blood. He then pulled the arm straight and the bone back through the wound to its place. They bound it securely with a bandage made from Martha's apron. The Indian said to Martha:

"You must go for the doctor, and I will carry him to your father's house."

The home was two miles away and over rough mountain paths. Martha was gone in a moment, and

116

the Indian sat waiting for Julian to regain consciousness. He very soon opened his eyes, and not seeing
Martha, asked where she was. Wilson told him she
had gone for the doctor, and that he would carry him
to the house.

"How can you do that over these mountain
roads?" said Julian.

"You must assist me some. You must put your
good arm around my neck and I will take you on my
back, if you can hold on. I can carry you safely."

"I want you," said Julian, "to make me a vow
that you will not tell anything about our fight or the
cause of it till I recover."

"If," said Wilson, "you will promise me you will
not cross Martha's path again, and let her be happy
in her own home, I will keep your secret."

"I promise I will not make her unhappy if I can
help it."

"I accept your promise; but beware! if you wrong
her I will kill you!"

Julian having recovered somewhat, Wilson took
him on his back and carried him safely out of the
mountain to James Thompson's cabin. The doctor
and Martha were not long in arriving. The fracture
and the wound were bad ones, but in due course of
time Julian was able to be moved to his home, where
he made a good recovery. Martha nursed him pa-

tiently and faithfully while he was in her father's house.

During Julian's stay, as he watched the beautiful, graceful and innocent girl, as she moved about the house, anticipating his every want and comfort, and when he remembered his present affliction was the result of the foul plot to ruin her beautiful young life, he cursed himself and blessed Wilson Guy for saving him from himself, and her from the trap he had set for her destruction.

While he was at home he disclosed to his father and mother his determination to marry Martha Thompson. They were surprised and indignant, but he was inflexible in his purpose. The sham license was changed for a genuine one, and Martha Thompson became the bride of Julian Guthrie. Instead of putting the ocean between them he took her with him to Germany as his wife.

They remained in Europe three years, and when they returned all the shyness of the mountain girl had disappeared, and Julian Guthrie had the most beautiful and attractive wife in all this country, and he became one of the most substantial and reliable men in the State.

Wilson Guy, the hermit hunter and half-breed Indian, still lives, and loves and worships in the lonely cove in Iron Mountain, and is a frequent visitor to the home of Julian, and though fond of telling of his numerous adventures, has never from that day to this referred to this incident.

Mr. Guthrie, however, on all occasions laughs and tells how " Wilson whipped a college sport into manhood."

THE MEANEST MAN IN THE WORLD

TWENTY-FIVE years ago Mattie French was a beautiful, fascinating girl—a reigning belle. She was not only beautiful in person, but had charming manners, and possessed a lovely character. Though she was a leader of social life, she was also the friend of those in the humbler walks of life. Wherever there was comfort or aid required, there Mattie French was to be found.

Being universally admired by men, it was commonly considered that she could have her choice of any of her admirers whenever she would consent to marry. Everybody was amazed when it was rumored that she was engaged to Frank Marks, a man without character or occupation, a drinking man and a gambler. No argument or warning served to change her decision, so she married Frank Marks. It was a repetition of the same old story. Mrs. Marks was never heard to complain or regret her choice, though there had been threats to lynch Marks for his brutal treatment of his wife.

In the month of February, one Sunday night about one o'clock (I distinctly remember the month, because it was spring weather, although still winter) the town had grown quiet and the people had gone to rest. The moonbeams behind the fleecy clouds made them look light as they flew before a strong gale. At intervals the face of the moon would show through a rift in the clouds. On that day they had heard the oft-repeated words, " Blessed are the meek, for they shall inherit the earth," " Blessed are the peacemakers, for they shall be called the children of God," and other beatitudes. But the same fierce struggle for supremacy that has been going on ever since the mother of Zebedee's children said unto the Master: " Grant that these my two sons may sit, the one on Thy right hand, and the other on Thy left, in Thy Kingdom," was to begin at dawn.

I had just returned to my office from one of the most pathetic scenes I had ever witnessed, and was disturbed mentally, physically and spiritually. Mrs. Marks had exclaimed as I entered her room: " Oh, my God! my poor babe is dying! How can I ever give her up ? " There was all the anguish of a broken heart embraced in her words. " Suffer the little children to come unto me, and forbid them not, for of such is the Kingdom of God," was the only reply I could make, for the little sufferer had already obeyed the summons. The poor mother held only the lifeless body of her babe.

The silence grew oppressive; the flickering shadows on the wall made by a coal oil lamp without a chimney gave the silent mother a deathly pallor.

"Mrs. Marks," I said, "let me lay the little body in the cradle." There was no reply. I repeated the question. Still she made no response. I then went to her and was shocked to find that she had followed her babe to the very gate of Heaven. I did not move then, but went softly out, closed the door, and left them to welcome the drunken, brutal husband when he returned. Happily they were beyond his curses and abuse, and I hoped the shock might bring him to his senses. Returning to my office, I threw myself on a couch, and was soon asleep and did not wake until called to breakfast.

While eating at the table I glanced over the morning paper, and saw in big headlines: "Mrs. Marks and Baby Murdered Last Night by Her Drunken Husband! Marks Arrested and in Jail. Has Made Full Confession of the Horrible Crime!"

I was dumbfounded at this statement. Why should Marks have confessed to the murder of his wife and child? The notice read that Marks in his confession had stated that he came home drunk and found his wife sitting in a chair with the baby in her lap. He had asked her for food, and she made no reply. He again demanded something to eat, and still she made no reply. He became enraged and struck her on the head with a club, and kicked at her after she had fallen, and in so doing accidentally kicked the baby. Marks had been found asleep in an adjoining room, and the mother and babe dead on the floor. The inquest was to be held at nine o'clock that morning.

Promptly at nine o'clock I went to the house, having resolved that at present I would say nothing. No one had seen me enter the house or leave it. I waited to see what the inquest would develop. The jurors were duly sworn, and there were but two witnesses. A neighbor to Mrs. Marks testified " That she knew Mrs. Marks' babe was sick, and had gone in early in the morning to see about it, and had found them both dead on the floor, and Marks in an adjoining room in bed with his clothes and boots on. She was afraid to wake him, and had called in a policeman, who found everything as she had stated."

The policeman testified that he had awakened Marks out of a drunken slumber, and asked him why he had been beating his wife? He repeated that he had struck her only once because she would not give him any supper. He said he did not intend to kick the baby; he kicked at his wife and struck the baby, but had not hurt it for it did not cry. The policeman asked him what he had struck his wife with, and Marks replied, "With a club." When asked if he had hurt her much, he replied that he thought not as he had often struck her harder than that. The policeman then asked him if he knocked her down. He replied that she had fallen out of the chair to keep him from striking her any more, but that he had not struck her hard. He was then told he had struck hard enough to break her skull, and had kicked the baby hard enough to kill it, and that they were both dead on the floor.

This seemed to bring Marks to his senses. " Impossible," he cried, and rushing into the room, he gazed terror-stricken at his wife and child as they lay dead on the floor. Then he cried out: " My God! I have murdered my wife and babe." Marks was placed under arrest by the policeman and taken to jail.

Marks made this same statement. The case was so plain that no other witnesses were called. The prisoner was remanded to jail to await the action of the grand jury. In due course the grand jury found a true bill for murder in the first degree. He was tried, convicted and sentenced to be hanged on the twenty-second day of March. There appeared to be absolutely no extenuating circumstances, since Marks had admitted that he knew what he was doing when he struck his wife.

The day for the execution arrived, and I sent for the Commonwealth's Attorney and told him to wire the Governor for a reprieve, as I had positive evidence that Marks did not murder his wife and child. He was thunderstruck and wanted to know what the evidence was. I told him they had both died from natural causes, that I was present and witnessed their deaths.

" Doctor, you are under the influence of an opiate. You are dreaming. It is impossible that you saw these people die, when Marks has confessed to having killed them."

" Yes," said I, " he has not only confessed, but in the very depths of his soul believes, that he murdered them. But they were dead when he came home; dead when he struck his wife."

I again related all the circumstances and convinced him of the truth of my statement.

He telegraphed the Governor that new evidence had been discovered, and to stay the execution until it could be investigated. At the last moment a message staying the execution was received. The case was reopened and I satisfied the court and jury that Frank Marks did not murder his wife and babe, and he was acquitted. He was more rejoiced to know he had not murdered them than he was to escape the gallows.

" How can I ever thank you or show my debt of gratitude ? " he exclaimed, his voice trembling with deep emotion. " The debt can never in this world be paid by words or by deeds. I am willing to be your slave the remainder of my days."

The shock accomplished my purpose; it made a

sober man of Marks. He was never known to take another drink, and became prosperous in business. Years after I had reverses and was hard pressed for money. I had a note against Marks for sixty dollars, for medical services which I had rendered him in a serious case of illness. His life had been saved only by my careful attention, and the faithful, patient nursing of his wife. I presented the note to him for payment, and though abundantly able to pay it, he refused to do so unless I would deduct the interest. This I declined to do. He then pleaded statute of limitation on the note and evaded payment.